Anthony Burgess

Chatsky and
Miser, Miser!

Two Plays

Edited by Andrew Biswell

Salamander Street

PLAYS

Published in 2023 by Salamander Street Ltd., a Wordville imprint,
(info@salamanderstreet.com).

Chatsky © The International Anthony Burgess Foundation 1993, 2023.

Miser, Miser! © The International Anthony Burgess Foundation 1991, 2023.

Introduction © Andrew Biswell 2023.

PB ISBN: 9781914228889

E ISBN: 9781914228308

10 9 8 7 6 5 4 3 2 1

Further copies of this publication can be purchased from
www.salamanderstreet.com

Wordville

Contents

Introduction

by Andrew Biswell

CHATSKY, Alexander Griboyedov's verse comedy in four acts, is one of the most popular and most often quoted plays in Russia, but it is almost unknown to English-speaking audiences. Anthony Burgess aimed to change that. A gifted linguist who listed his hobbies as 'wife, language-learning' in *Who's Who*, Burgess taught himself Russian in six weeks in 1961, shortly before he visited Leningrad to gather material for his novel, *A Clockwork Orange*. He had enough Russian to be able to read Pushkin and Pasternak, and he maintained friendships with dissident Russian writers and publishers during the Soviet era. Apart from a few short poems, *Chatsky* is the most substantial piece of translation work that Burgess undertook from Russian. One of his reasons for wanting to make an English version, preserving the strict rhymes of the original play, was that everyone told him it could not be done.

No doubt Burgess was attracted to Griboyedov's work because he recognised something of himself, both in the figure of the author and in the character of Chatsky. Born in or around 1795, Griboyedov was a serious musician who wrote piano music and composed musical comedies in his youth. After a wound to his hand, sustained during a duel, ended his career as a pianist, he joined the diplomatic service in 1818. Posted to Chechnya and Persia, he returned to Moscow in 1823 and submitted *Chatsky* to the tsarist censors. The play was immediately banned, but it was rumoured that up to 40,000 copies were circulating in manuscript. By the time *Chatsky* was performed in 1833, Griboyedov was already dead: he was murdered, along with all but one of his diplomatic colleagues, when an angry mob stormed the Russian embassy in Tehran in 1829. He was thirty-four years old.

The play is set in Moscow in the early 1820s, roughly ten years after the fire which had destroyed most of the city in 1812. Chatsky, a young intellectual, returns to Moscow after an absence of three years and proposes to his old flame, Sophia, the daughter of Famusov, a government official. But Sophia is now in love with Molchalin, her father's secretary, and she rejects him. In a series of comic encounters, Chatsky crosses swords with various characters who are assembling in Famusov's house for a party. In an age where tactfulness and sycophancy are the rule, he seems to be the only man who is willing to speak truth to power.

i

There's a strong echo, in this English version, of Cyrano de Bergerac, the hero of Edmond Rostand's nineteenth-century play, which Burgess had translated for the Tyrone Guthrie Theater in America in 1971. When Michael Langham directed Christopher Plummer in the role of Cyrano at the Guthrie, he said that the character reminded him of Burgess himself in his dogged refusal to bite his tongue and kowtow to the powerful.

Chatsky was performed at the Almeida Theatre in Islington from 11 March to 24 April 1993, featuring Colin Firth as Chatsky and Jemma Redgrave as Sophia, in a production directed by Jonathan Kent. Burgess, who was already very unwell with the lung cancer that was to end his life, met the cast and director on the opening night.

Reviewing the play, Jack Tinker wrote in the *Daily Mail*: 'Not for many a bleak night have we been bowled away by words of such bold and witty poetry [...] Thanks to Anthony Burgess's volatile and muscular verse translation, plus the ongoing vision of this tiny North London theatre, we have an old master miraculously brought to new life.' Nicholas de Jongh in the *Evening Standard* was more sceptical, describing the play as 'tame and toothless.'

Writing in *The Spectator*, Sheridan Morley said: 'Colin Firth has some difficulty letting us understand why Chatsky has always been regarded as the Russian Hamlet, but there are some magical supporting performances from the best cast of character actors in town.' Benedict Nightingale in *The Times* drew attention to the staging: 'malicious gossips mingle with blimps and fools; twittering princesses wobble about the stage like tiny pink blancmanges; and all the guests end up crowded together in a venomous frieze, screeching insults at Firth's Chatsky, exuding his usual earnest charm.'

Several critics commented on the quality of Burgess's adaptation. Michael Billington in *The Guardian* welcomed this new translation: 'Burgess pummels the air with puns and conceits so that a dumbo officer, whom Famusov hopes to pair off with Sophie, is characterised as "an empty nut and still they call him Colonel" and prompts Chatsky to ask "How about that other brilliant claimant, / That cerebral nullity in army raiment?" This is language sent on a drunken, headlong spree.' After its initial run at the Almeida, the production went on a three-month tour to theatres in Oxford, Richmond, Brighton, Newcastle, Malvern and Bath.

The original title of Griboyedov's play is *Gore ot Uma*, which translates as 'The Misery of Intelligence'. Most of the existing English translations are titled 'Woe From Wit' or 'Woe Out of Wit', although Vladimir Nabokov suggested 'Brains Hurt' as a possible alternative. Burgess follows an earlier translator, Joshua Cooper, in naming his version of the play after its principal character – but he adds a subtitle, 'The Importance of Being Stupid', which takes us into the realm of Oscar Wilde, one of his favourite dramatists. 'Being stupid,' according to Burgess, 'is what comedy is all about.' Some commentators have objected that Burgess deviates too far from the Russian source material, but the aim of his translation was to present a readable and actable text which would resonate with English-speaking audiences. Perhaps because of the invective of its hyper-articulate main character, Burgess maintained that *Chatsky* is one of the few really good comedies ever written for the stage.

Griboyedov tells us in his letters that he had made a careful study of Molière, and others have noticed that Chatsky bears a resemblance to Alceste, the ranting outsider who appears in *Le Misanthrope*. Neither of these characters is able to contain their rage against a society they view as hypocritical, and they say exactly what is on their minds, paying no regard to the conventional social decencies. Curiously, of all Molière's characters, the one Griboyedov liked the least was Harpagon in *The Miser*. In a letter to his friend Katenin, he wrote: 'I loathe caricature [...] *Le Bourgeois Gentilhomme* and *Le Malade Imaginaire* are portraits, excellent ones; *L'Avare* is an anthropos that he has manufactured himself – and insufferable.'

Not much is known about the history of *Miser, Miser!*, Burgess's version of Molière's well-known comedy, first performed in French in 1668. Following the success of the Royal Shakespeare Company's production of *Cyrano de Bergerac* in 1985, the director Terry Hands invited Burgess to make another translation from the French, and *Miser, Miser!* seems to have been intended as a script for Hands and his company. Why the play was never staged remains a mystery, although this may be connected to Hands's decision to step down as the RSC's artistic director in 1986. It is still awaiting its first performance.

Burgess's translation is unusual in that it is written in a mixture of prose and rhyming couplets, whereas the original French play is written entirely in prose. It's likely that Burgess was trying to recapture the tone of his verse translation of *Cyrano de Bergerac* – a commercial and critical triumph which has frequently been revived in London and New York, most recently on Broadway, with Kevin Kline and Jennifer Garner in the leading roles.

As *Miser, Miser!* has never been published or performed, the text which survives in the Burgess Foundation's archive does not include a translator's introduction. Elsewhere in his critical writing, Burgess mentions his strong admiration for Richard Wilbur's translations of Molière, which he'd read with close attention. It's more than likely that he set himself the task of trying to imagine what *The Miser* might have looked like if Wilbur had put it into English.

Taken together, these two previously unpublished plays underline the importance of theatre and poetry in the final phase of Burgess's career. His novels about poets and playwrights are already well known: Shakespeare in *Nothing Like the Sun*, John Keats in *ABBA ABBA*, Christopher Marlowe in *A Dead Man in Deptford*, and the fictional poet-musician Michael Byrne in *Byrne*, his posthumously-published verse novel about the pleasures and perils of leading an artistic life. Burgess published his earliest poems while he was still at school, and he continued to practice his technique over the next fifty years. *Chatsky* and *Miser, Miser!* remind us that this brilliant writer began and ended his artistic life as a poet.

The publication of these two late plays in verse brings the last period of his creative life more clearly into focus. Readers and actors will find much to surprise and delight them in these pages.

Andrew Biswell

Manchester

2023

Andrew Biswell is Professor of Modern Literature at Manchester Metropolitan University and Director of the International Anthony Burgess Foundation.

FURTHER READING

Joshua Cooper (translator), *The Government Inspector and Other Russian Plays* (Penguin Classics, 1990)

Alexander Griboedov, *Woe from Wit*, trans. Betty Hullick (Columbia University Press, 2020)

Edmond Rostand, *Cyrano de Bergerac*, translated and adapted by Anthony Burgess (Hutchinson, 1985)

Sophocles, *Oedipus the King*, trans. Anthony Burgess (Minnesota University Press, 1972)

CHATSKY
or
THE IMPORTANCE OF BEING STUPID

A Verse Comedy in Four Acts
by Alexander Sergeyevich Griboyedov

Translation
by Anthony Burgess

How ghastly every wise man's prospects are –
Woe comes from wit, or *góre ot umá*.

Foreword

by Anthony Burgess

ALEXANDER SERGEYEVICH GRIBOYEDOV (accent on the *yed*) sent
this play to the Imperial Censor in St Petersburg in 1824. He had been
working on it for some years, in the intervals of diplomatic work in
the Caucasus and Persia (now Iran). The play was promptly banned,
though permission was given for the publication of a few harmless
extracts in a magazine devoted to the theatre. After the upheaval of
a revolution in France and a French invasion of Russia, there was a
powerful desire to maintain a torpid stasis in Russian society.

Change, it was argued, was always dangerous. The Czar, Alexander I, had
known a period of youthful liberalism, but he had now taken refuge
from the perilously mobile world in religious mysticism. While the
government tried to maintain Russian society as a kind of barbarous
autocracy, with no attempt to extirpate the feudal abomination of
serfdom, officers in the Russian Army that had fought Napoleon had
been strongly influenced by the civilised Europe that had been beaten
back from the gates of Moscow in 1812.

It was in 1812 that Griboyedov, at the age of seventeen, abandoned
his university education in Moscow and took a commission in the
Hussars. With the war over, the desire for adventure led him into the
Foreign Service. He had studied classical and modern languages but
now became proficient in Arabic and Persian. His talents were varied
and, so his junior contemporary Pushkin believed, more considerable
than was proper for one young man. He was a fine pianist and even a
moderate composer. While he was living in St Petersburg he pursued
the artistic, social and diplomatic activities appropriate to his talents
and status, writing light theatrical entertainments, loving the company
of actors, singers and dancers. There was a ballerina named Istomina,
mentioned in Pushkin's *Eugene Onegin*, with whom Griboyedov grew
friendly – apparently platonically – but the friendship led him into a
duel from which he emerged whole, except for a wound in the little
fingers intended to ruin his pianistic prowess. Because of the scandal
ensuing on the duel, he was posted to Teheran in 1819, maintaining
close links with Persian culture.

He came back to St Petersburg on a long leave in 1823, visiting
Moscow to renew his acquaintance with the types satirised in this play.

Finished, the play, though banned, was not completely suppressed. Manuscript copies were made of it: it is said that more than 40,000 of these were in circulation. After an arrest on the charge of participating in the failed Decembrist mutiny against the new Czar, Nicholas I, long interrogation and eventual release, he was sent back to Iran and the Caucasus. A Russo-Persian war of great ferocity broke out, and Griboyedov was instrumental in negotiating the peace, in which the harsh terms of the Treaty of Turkmanchai were imposed on a resentful Persia. He was chosen to carry the engrossed document of the Treaty to St Petersburg, where gun salutes and decorations greeted him, as well as a purse crammed with gold. Despite his desire to retire and devote himself to literature, the Czar insisted on his returning to Teheran. Griboyedov was rightly reluctant to go back, being aware of numerous Persian enemies, but the journey was mollified by his marriage to Princess Nina Chavchavadze, the sixteen-year-old daughter of a Georgian general and poet who was nationally famous. The bride was of great beauty, and the honeymoon was blissful. The honeymoon was about all there was of the marriage. She went with him as far as Tabriz; he went on to Teheran without her. Rightly.

For trouble was not long in coming. An Armenian eunuch came to the Russian legation, seeking asylum – justly, since the province of Erivan where he had been born had recently been ceded to Russia. Two Armenian girls who had escaped from the Shah's son-in-law's harem made a similar claim to be considered subjects of the Czar. Griboyedov not only granted refuge to these but began to look around for other disgruntled infidels who resented Muslim tyranny. It was on 30 January 1829 that a crowd of Islamic fanatics invaded the Teheran legation and slaughtered Griboyedov and all of his staff save one. His mutilated body was identifiable from the duelling scar on his little finger. He was only thirty-four years old.

His literary remains are few, but the comedy entitled *Gore ot Uma* is considered to be a masterpiece. In 1833 it was presented in Moscow, heavily cut but recognisable as distinguished satire with a rather odd flavour. In 1861 the old restrictions were lifted, and the entire text was published for the first time. It has remained in the Russian repertory ever since, acknowledged to be a virtuoso vehicle for male actors, a source of quotations, both conscious and not, and a damnably difficult play to translate.

The verse form is strange – rhyme, lines of variable length though always iambic – and the flavour far from poetic. Verse, on the stage, as T.S. Eliot has shown, can lift from banality the colloquial and naturalistic: it is a medium for the exploitation of rhythm rather than a vessel for the profound or colourful. It is difficult to imagine *Gore ot Uma* as a prose production. I know of no English translation previous to the one here offered except that of Joshua Cooper, who had his own prosodic reasons for a kind of free verse without rhyme. His version is, I think, unactable, though he has some good pentametric lines, one or two of which I have appropriated here. He was a much better Russian scholar than I can ever hope to be, and his translation perhaps suffers by being too close to the original.

My concern is to maintain such closeness as is compatible with a visible acting version, but a number of Griboyedov's references cannot be well understood without special historical indoctrination, and generalities have occasionally been substituted for baffling particulars. The rough rhyming couplets I have used belong to a fairly recent theatrical tradition – one in which rhymed French plays have been rendered into a form less rigid than the English Restoration stage was prepared to accept, and the renderings have achieved a certain commercial success. I am thinking of Richard Wilbur's versions of Molière and my own adaptation of Rostand's *Cyrano de Bergerac*.

The play must always seem topical, since it is about the failed attempt of an intellectual rebel to indent the smug and philistine society in which he finds himself. He comes from his travels to a depraved city, rants, raves, is disappointed bitterly in love, then goes off again. Everything is confined, following the classical tradition, to a single day and a single place. The concision is admirable, and though the characters are more types than individuals they are sufficiently alive. This is comedy, but comedy of considerable bitterness. Its flavour is not of a kind to be found much outside Russia. As there are few enough good comedies in the world, it is important that this be not merely known about and read but also enstaged.

The title is a problem. Gore ot Uma has been translated as 'Woe Out Of Wit', or 'Bitterness Out Of Intelligence'. To give the play the name of its protagonist – Chatsky – is not perhaps helpful. I deliberately evoke the title of Wilde's great comedy in 'The Importance Of Being Stupid', which is what the comedy is about. The situation it depicts is an eternal one.

A.B.
St Margarets
Easter Day 1991

7

CHATSKY was first performed at Almeida Theatre in London on 11th March 1993, directed by Jonathan Kent. The cast was as follows:

Liza	Minnie Driver
Sophie	Jemma Redgrave
Famusov	Dinsdale Landen
Molchalin	Jonathan Cullen
Peter, a servant	Sean Harris
Chatsky	Colin Firth
Colonel Skalozub	John Fortune
Nathalie Gorich	Delia Lindsay
Gorich	Bob Goody
Prince Tugo-Ukhovsky	Graham Lines
Princess Tugo-Ukhovsky	Helen Lindsay
Princess	Rebecca Harries
Princess	Rachel Lumberg
Princess	Anna Mackmin
Princess	Caroline Ryder
Princess	Morag Siller
Countess Khryumina	Jane Freeman
Countess Khryumina	Sarah Crowden
Zagoretsky	Murray Melvin
Miss Khylostova	Rosalind Knight
Girl	Ashabi Ajikawo/Sebrina Modest
Mr N	John Tordoff
Mr D	Laurance Rudic
Repetilov	David O'Hara

Characters

PAVEL FAMUSOV, director of a Government office

SOPHIE, his daughter

LIZA, Sophie's maid

ALEXIS MOLCHALIN, Famusov's secretary

ALEXANDER CHATSKY

COLONEL SERGE SKALOZUB

NATHALIE AND PLATO GORICH

PRINCE TUGO-UKHOVSKY

THE PRINCESS, his wife

THEIR SIX DAUGHTERS

COUNTESS KHRYUMINA, a grandmother

COUNTESS KHRYUMINA, her granddaughter

ANTHONY ZAGORETSKY, a rogue

MISS KHYLOSTOVA, Famusov's sister-in-law

MR N, MR D, Guests at Famusov's party

REPETILOV

SERVANTS

The action takes place on a single winter's day at Famusov's house in Moscow, in the early 1820s.

Act One

The drawing room at first light. A huge grandfather clock that plays a tune on the hour.
LIZA, *the maid, wakes suddenly in a rather uncomfortable wooden chair.*

LIZA: It's getting light. Didn't the night go quick!

I miss my bed. But here I had to stick,

Stuck in this chair. And sort of keeping guard.

The damned seat slopes a lot. The damned thing's hard.

To make me drop off, see, if I drop off.

I dropped off without dropping off. A cough,

A sneeze in the sky says morning. And it's cold,

Pure Moscow cold. Oh God, they've got to be told.

Miss! Miss! Miss Sophie! It's not right.

You've been at what you've been at all the night.

You too, Mr Molchalin. Deaf. And daft.

I gave fair warning but they only laughed.

Ought to be scared. There's one you didn't invite

Ready to come and you know who. Not right.

Break it up in there. Love. So they say.

I ought to get a bit of extra pay

For what she's getting. Come on. Have a bit

Of sense. Your dad'll be here.

SOPHIE: *(off)*   What time is it?

LIZA: Everyone's up.

SOPHIE: The time?

LIZA: It's after six,

11

Or seven. Or eight.

SOPHIE: Nonsense.

LIZA: Nonsense! I'll fix

Their nonsense. None so deaf as those that won't –

Here. I'll get them out, see if I don't.

She puts the hour hand of the clock to the hour, and it discourses loud music. **FAMUSOV** *comes in.*

LIZA: Oh, the master.

FAMUSOV: Master. So it's yours.

I don't care much for early overtures.

I thought I'd heard a flute or a tin whistle

And the piano. But I said: Oh, this'll

Not be Sophie, not at this hour.

LIZA: Nor me.

It went off accidental, see.

FAMUSOV: I see.

He switches the noise off.

Accidental purpose. Naughty, aren't you?

Bad little baggage, eh?

He makes for her lecherously.

LIZA: Get off, you shan't, you

Ought to know your place.

FAMUSOV: All prim and proper,

But full of fun when you unscrew the stopper,

Eh?

LIZA:	You a gent, and getting on as well.
FAMUSOV:	Yes to the first.
LIZA:	Get away now, or I'll tell.
FAMUSOV:	Tell who? Sophie's asleep.
LIZA:	Just gone to bed.

Not dropped off yet.

FAMUSOV:	What?
LIZA:	Reading, so she said.

Said she was going to read a book in French.

All night, she said. Aloud.

FAMUSOV: The stupid wench.

She'll ruin her eyesight. Tell her that from me.

Besides, there's nothing in books. I see. I see.

With French books she can keep awake all night.

With Russian ones I go out like a light.

Interesting.

LIZA: Very, sir. I'll tell her that.

Soon as she's up. Now go. She's like a cat.

The least noise wakes her.

FAMUSOV: Yet your devoted labours

Put on that thing to wake her and the neighbours.

I don't get this.

LIZA: You won't get this. Now go.

Leave me alone.

FAMUSOV: Oh well –

LIZA: You ought to know

A young girl's sleep's as flimsy as shot silk.

Anything wakes her – clank of the morning milk,

Somebody's foot scrape scraping on a scraper,

The turning over of the morning paper.

They have to hear.

FAMUSOV: *You* have to spin your fibs.

SOPHIE: *(off)* Liza.

FAMUSOV: Shhhh.

He tiptoes out.

LIZA: Well, so much for his nibs.

His brain is going and the rest is gone.

The gentry carry on and carry on.

The first carry-on's with throat and tongue and teeth,

The other's what he carries underneath.

Gentry.

SOPHIE: *(entering)*   Liza, what was all that about?

LIZA: Whatever it was, it's got you lovebirds out.

MOLCHALIN *too comes in.*

Playing his flute or something all the night.

SOPHIE: And here's our enemy the morning light

Ripping the velvet darkness.

LIZA: Pine away.

Some has to watch all night and work all day.

I've done a day's work with your dad already.

You, sir, stiffen the rest of you. Come, steady –

Swallow the heart that's in your gob and bow

And go. You see that clock? You see it? Now

Look out of the window. All the world's clocked on.

Working away with half the morning gone.

SOPHIE: Happiness isn't measured by the clock.

LIZA: Don't bother then. There's me to take the knock

When the knock knocks.

SOPHIE: A wretched boring day –

Paws off. Mr Molchalin – on your way.

FAMUSOV *enters vigorously.*

FAMUSOV: Hallo, what's this? Molchalin, is this you?

You, at this hour. And little Sophie too.

I don't trust early risers. You. And her.

SOPHIE: He's just come in.

MOLCHALIN: From my constitutional, sir.

FAMUSOV: I don't like this. Out of your bed you roll,

And there he is, fresh from a morning stroll.

And so you meet. Oh yes, of course, by chance,

A sweet coincidental circumstance.

What are girls coming to? I blame the French,

Filling our streets up with the stink and stench

Of Paris perfumes, bookshops with their novels.

Everyone scoffs snails, everyone grovels

Before the frogs. This fashion – do you stock it?

The ruination of the heart and pocket.

French hat-shops, dress-shops, cake-shops, filthy dances,

And all these damned insomniac romances –

Reading of love and lechery all night,

Wasting your time as well as candlelight,

French underwear and overwear – coiffures.

"I'll have a vodka" – "Really?" – "And what's yours?"

"Oh, water if it comes from the Paris sewers."

The French! We kicked them out, and serve them right.

SOPHIE: Papa, papa, you gave me such a fright,

Barging in here so early in the morning,

As burly as a bear, no word, no warning.

It startled me, the way you lumbered in.

My pulse is pounding, head's all in a spin.

FAMUSOV: Bounding in like a bear, eh? Sorry, I'm sure.

Frightened you, did I? Girl, you moan of your

Raw nerves. How would you like mine, eh?

Clawing like a Siberian cat all day

At documents, at depositions, dockets,

And pawers with petitions in their pockets,

Trying to do my duty to the Czar.

You just don't know what high-class worries are.

And now – I get deceived.

SOPHIE: *(distraught)* By whom, papa?

FAMUSOV: Crying, is it – at my unreasonableness?

Scolding you, am I? I suppose that croak means yes.

All right, take a deep breath. Listen now

To my recapu whatsit. Think of how

I brought you up. Your mother in the grave,

You in the cradle. Poor girl. How I gave

No thought to anything except yes, you.

I found that Madame Rosier for you, who

Was like a second mother, yes, she was.

Or might have been. She only left because

Somebody offered her five hundred more.

Money – that's all that some of them go for.

Such principles she had, a real right measure

Of love – well paid for, blast her. A real treasure.

Forget her. Never mind about Madame.

Your father is your mother now. I am

A model, independent, my own master,

A desirable widower, who's greying faster,

I must admit, than is proper to my youth,

Sort of. I live clean too. That's the truth.

LIZA: If I might put a word in.

FAMUSOV: You be quiet.

And now – this generation – rot and riot,

Lechery, luxury, I don't know what.

And daughters are the worst ones of the lot.

Penniless foreigners come to this city,

Dagoes and frogs. We take them out of pity

Into our households, employing them as tutors

To decent Russian girls. They become suitors,

As if their trade of teaching song and dance –

The only things they've brought with them from France –

Fitted the horrors to be sons-in-law.

And you, sir, wipe that smirk from your upper jaw.

You may be Russian but you're just as bad.

You were a nobody, a snot-nosed lad,

Until I dragged you from the Moscow mud.

You seem to think you're blessed with noble blood

The way you strut. You, sir, a Grade Eight clerk.

I raised you shivering from the dirty dark

To be my secretary. Don't forget it.

SOPHIE: Why do you rage like that, papa? You let it

Blow you up like a bullfrog.

FAMUSOV: Oh, is that so?

SOPHIE: This poor young man lodges in this palazzo.

He works for you so wanted to be near,

He was making for his room but landed here.

FAMUSOV: Meant to land here. A nice smug little islet,

A straight passage and a shifty pilot.

SOPHIE: Coincidence. I heard you here with Liza,

Booming away. It opened up my eyes, a

Big cold douche. And so I rushed right in.

FAMUSOV: Add to the inventory another sin.

I made an indiscreet and shocking choice

Selecting the wrong time to use my voice.

SOPHIE: A girl can easily get scared when she

Has had a nightmare. Listen, and you'll see

Why I was scared.

FAMUSOV: *(sitting down resignedly)*

All right, get on with it.

SOPHIE: There was this flowery meadow, all sunlit.

I wandered through it, doing some botany,

And who should be there, standing over me,

But someone smiling, kind, and all alone,

The sort you meet and feel you've always known,

But shy, you know, ill-dressed and very poor.

FAMUSOV: Enough, my girl. I don't want any more.

Won't have you dreaming of <u>poor</u> sons of bitches.

SOPHIE: The sky dissolved, the meadow and its riches,

And we were in a dark room with no door.

And then you suddenly burst up from the floor,

As pale as putty, with your hair on end.

Then there's a crash. Between me and my friend

Things – beasts not people – hairy, dim, grim,

Grab him with claws and start to torture him,

Him, my dream man, my walking treasure chest.

I try to get to him, protect, protest,

But you drag me back while all those monsters roar

And laugh and jeer and scream. He's there no more.

Only his voice, fainter and fainter calling.

Then I wake up, to hear you, thumping, bawling.

Why so early, I wonder. I rise and see

You, her, him. And now there's me.

FAMUSOV: A full-dress sort of dream, with devils of hell

But no deceit, so far as I can tell.

But you, how about you?

MOLCHALIN: I heard your voice, sir.

FAMUSOV: Lovely. A song to make the day rejoice, sir.

A kind of muezzin from a minaret,

Calling the faithful. And you make a dead set

In my direction. Wonderful. But why?

MOLCHALIN: I've got these papers, sir.

FAMUSOV: Oh, let me die.

I've seen a miracle. Such zeal and zest

For paperwork. Sophie, run off and rest,

Sleep off that nightmare. There's queer things in dreams

And queerer in real life. Or so it seems.

He loves his paperwork. And what was it you said?

You looked for flowers and found a friend instead.

Empty your head of it. Get back to bed.

Let's see those papers.

MOLCHALIN: Sir, I thought you'd better

Revise what's in this ministerial letter.

There's an inconsistency. And this grammar looks –

Well – awkward, sir.

FAMUSOV: Grammar's for grammar books,

And the first rule is: when a thing is signed,

It's signed. And when it's signed it's off your mind.

The second rule of the bureaucratic caper

Is to get rid of – not to pile up – paper.

Come on.

They leave, **FAMUSOV** *pushing* **MOLCHALIN** *ahead.*

LIZA: Fun, wasn't it? Well, not much fun.

It isn't funny what we've been and done.

Sin is all right – the crackling on the pork.

It's tasty, sin. Till people start to talk.

SOPHIE: Well, let them talk. And let them scream and shout.

Papa's the only one to scream about.

Small-minded. Stubborn. Never known to budge.

Always like that. Now you yourself can judge.

LIZA: Oh yes, I can. He wants his way all right.

It was a bit dangerous, you know, last night.

Suppose he locks you up. If I'm there with you

You'll have some company. But what'll you do

If me and Molchalin get chucked out in the street?

SOPHIE: Luck's a strange thing. Some fall on their feet

And others on the other thing. Worse than me,

A lot of them, and get away scot-free.

There we were making music, making love.

Time disappeared. Slid by. There was no doubt of

Fate being on our side. Absolute bliss,

But we were riding towards a precipice.

LIZA: You never listen, do you? Told you so

Is what I never tell you. I said: no,

No good will come of it. You heard. Instead

Of someone that you fancy, like I said,

Your dad requires a fancy son-in-law,

One of these Moscow swells that go haw-haw,

With half a ton of medals and a sash,

And half a pound of wax on his moustache.

But the more medals often the less cash.

He wants them both, medals and marble halls,

Banquets and bubbly and blooming balls.

Balls is the word. There's Colonel Skalozub

For instance, with his whiskers like a shrub

But tubs of money, and he's going to be

A general.

SOPHIE: General. Think of the fun for me,

Droning about tactics and strategy,

And lines and columns – like a daily journal.

An empty nut and yet they call him colonel.

Curried complexion and a hobnailed liver.

I'd rather chuck myself in Moscow river.

LIZA:
It's military intelligence makes a general,

Different, they say, from human and animal.

Funny, there's Mr Chatsky on my mind

These last few days. Where are you going to find

A man like Mr Chatsky? Well, not here,

Although I hear things. Must be three years near

He's been away. Don't want to rake old coals,

But what they call a joining up of souls

Seemed like it was on the cards.

SOPHIE:
                                    Could I forget?

There was no one like him. Witty and gay and yet

Unkind – very. He flouted the social rules

And made the rest of us think we were fools.

LIZA:
You forget the main thing. When he said goodbye

There was a river streaming from each eye.

Come on, cheer up, I said. Life is for giggles.

And then he wipes his face and sniffs and wriggles

And says: It's not for nothing that I'm grieving,

Dear Liza. God alone knows what I'm leaving

Or what I'll find when I get back. Pathetic.

And, when you come to think of it –

SOPHIE:
                                    Prophetic?

My heart's my own, so please don't peek inside it.

I may have been a fool – have I denied it?

Sometimes I blame myself – ask did I break

Faith. Was I fickle? Perhaps the real mistake

Was taking him for granted. We grew up

Together, sipping from a nursery cup

A childhood life in common. When he was older

He gave my company a coldish shoulder.

He kept away. But when he came back later

It was with love – a gush from a long-dead crater,

The big imperious lover, very touchy,

Very demanding, wanting far too much. He

Was witty, clever, brilliant, and he knew it.

He picked his friends like raisins out of suet,

Then thought himself too big for our milieu,

So off he goes, a world-wide traveller.

In love, he says, and so he has to travel.

There is a mystery I can't unravel.

LIZA: They say he had to travel far and wide

To find a cure for something wrong inside,

Taking the waters, able to afford 'em,

But I believe his main complaint was –

SOPHIE: Boredom.

His only happiness is in derision.

There's nothing much romantic in his vision.

The man I love is not like him a bit,

He lacks no love although he lacks quick wit.

Unselfish, modest, giving no offence,

Bashful even. Though his love's intense

It overflows in saying he adores me.

He bores my eyes with his but never bores me.

We were together till the sun arose.

What do you think we were doing?

LIZA:
                                        Heaven knows.

It's not my place even to think it, miss.

SOPHIE: He took my hand, again, again, like this

And pressed it to his heart.

LIZA:
                                        And you took his

And pressed it to the place where *your* heart is.

SOPHIE: No, pure holy communion, eye to eye,

Bosom to bosom. Now you're guffawing. Why?

LIZA: Sorry. I was thinking of that aunt you had.

There was this French gardener, just a lad,

That ran away. She'd really got it bad.

She forgot to dye her hair, and three days after

– Grey as a badger.

SOPHIE:
                                I suppose I'll earn your laughter

When I go grey of disappointed love.

LIZA: Sorry, miss. I was only trying to shove

You out of the miseries.

A SERVANT *comes in, announces, leaves.*

SERVANT:
                                Mr Chatsky.

SOPHIE: No!

CHATSKY *enters impetuously.*

CHATSKY: The sun's up. But you cast a fierier glow

                On this your servant, kneeling at your feet –

                Figuratively speaking. Come, a kiss. We meet

                After an endless parting. Were you not

                Expecting me? Not one solitary jot

                Of pleasure? Just a cold trickle of surprise?

                Heat in your cheeks but not much in your eyes.

                One would think a week, even a day,

                Had passed, and we had bored the time away.

                Love, I expected love. Swiftly I come

                Wrapped in a traveller's delirium,

                Forty-five hours without a wink of sleep.

                Five hundred miles, my carriage buried deep

                In snow or lashed by blizzards, soaked in rain,

                Wheels broken, mended, broken. And my brain

                Dazed with desire to get to you. Devotion

                That's earned at least a modicum of emotion.

SOPHIE: Mr Chatsky, I'm very pleased to see you.

CHATSKY: That's something. But if you were me and me you,

                Would that be enough? How's one supposed to act

                When one is really pleased? Is it a fact

                That I've exposed myself to lethal immersion

                In icy rivers just for my own diversion?

LIZA:	Why, sir, you should have eavesdropped seconds ago.
	We were talking about you. Isn't that so?
SOPHIE:	Not only now. We talk about you always.
	See you in the shops, in streets, in hallways,
	Follow your shadow, look for your shadow in
	Travellers from foreign parts, ask if they've been
	Where you were, asked captains of foreign ships
	If they have seen your post-chaise on their trips.
CHATSKY:	I'd like to believe that, so believe I do.
	Blessed is the believer. What's not true
	Can still be – cosy. Well well, back again
	In Moscow. With you – you as you were then,
	Or not? Oh Lord, how innocent we were,
	Appearing, disappearing – here, then there,
	Romping around that table – and that chair.
	There sat your father, there that old madame
	Playing at piquet, while we used to cram
	Ourselves in that dark corner, safe secluded,
	Until a creak, a croak, a cough intruded.
SOPHIE:	Nursery days.
CHATSKY:	And now you're seventeen,
	Blossoming, all set to be a queen,
	Fascinating, fit to fire a poet,
	Inimitable, and by God you know it.
	That's why you're prim, stand-offish. You compel me

To ask if you're in love. Come on now, tell me.

Don't stop to think up something nice and plausible.

Don't get so flustered.

SOPHIE: Really, it's impossible

Not to get flustered when you stare like that,

Firing off questions.

CHATSKY: What else can I stare at

But lovely you? Moscow, of course, invites

Stares, so do the high-class Muscovites.

Gossip and love affairs. Tomorrow's ball,

The two last night – it soon begins to pall.

Moscow, beautiful Moscow, at a pinch'll

Do, I suppose, but God, it's so provincial.

SOPHIE: You've seen too much of the world. This running down

Of good old Moscow. Is there a better town?

CHATSKY: The best place is where none of us morons are.

But never mind. How is your dear Papa?

Still a staunch pillar of the English Club,

Giving the waitresses a friendly rub?

Your uncle – is he still rabbiting around?

Your foxy cousin – has he gone to ground?

How are our princes and our dear princesses –

Indulging still in philistine excesses,

Spending taxpayers' cash on caviare

And dancing where the latest cretins are?

How is our Minister of Education?

Still beaming over an unlettered nation?

The pillars of the Church – do they persist

In demonstrating God does not exist?

That lady writer whose patrician nose

Can't sniff the sad putridity of her prose,

Fodder for shopgirls that she's never met,

A doddering arbitress of etiquette.

I note a prevalence of pills and poxes,

And vagrants shivering in cardboard boxes

In hearing of the wrangling of the parties.

But still it's home – and home is where the heart is.

SOPHIE: You and my aunt should breakfast tкte a tкte.

You have a common taste in things to hate.

CHATSKY: Your aunt, I know, was rather good at hating

Ninety years a royal maid in waiting

And still a maid? Isn't she married yet?

She used to keep a panther as a pet

But now, I hear, it's pugs and unmarried mothers

And exiled Muslims. They are now our brothers,

I hear, revising Christian infamies,

Blessing our polygamic tendencies.

As for the Moscow dialect – my limbs

Go weak at its new-fangled acronyms.

SOPHIE: Well, you're the language man.

CHATSKY: I have a tongue –

Tart, but not pompous. Sorry if I've slung

More fatuities around than Whatsisname.

It's the excitement. Sorry just the same.

Where he is? Molchalin's who I mean,

The dumb obedient clerical machine

Who moons upon the flute. Not gay, not gallant,

And unequipped with even a minor talent.

Still, he'll get somewhere. Whatever he may lack,

He has the gift of never striking back.

SOPHIE: (He's not a human being. He's a snake.)

Have you, in irony or sheer mistake,

Ever said something kind about a person?

Perhaps you did when coddled by your nurse, an

Infant who knew only how to coo.

CHATSKY: This is pure vinegar, and new for you.

Don't go back to my days of immature

Niggling. You can be absolutely sure

Of what I feel for you. Black night, grey day,

The bells a-tinkle on the homeward sleigh,

Blinded by a desert of dead white,

Urging it on, urging it day and night

To get to you. I hear the whip still – Faster.

What do I find? A little saint of plaster,

Chill as the tundra. Yet I love, I love,

	Helplessly. Those I'm contemptuous of

Helplessly. Those I'm contemptuous of

I deride because they deserve derision.

And why? They are the obverse of your vision.

Do I really cut and smite and smart?

If so, it's out of rhythm with my heart.

I see the comic aside, that's all. I laugh

And then forget. But there's my other half,

The part that breathes devotion and desire.

So order me to leap into a fire

And I will go, gladly – as to a feast.

SOPHIA: (Licking his burns would shut his trap at least.)

FAMUSOV *comes in.*

FAMUSOV: Who's this then?

SOPHIE: It's the one I dreamt about.

She and **LIZA** *leave.*

FAMUSOV: Dream, dream? So the dream's working out,

Is it? But it's you, bolt from the blue.

Never a line, never a word. It's you.

My dear boy, delighted. Three years, is it?

And here you are – just like a casual visit.

I bet you've got some things to tell – real stuff,

Traveller's tales – I just can't get enough

Of those. Sit down.

CHATSKY: Grown pretty, hasn't she,

Your Sophie?

FAMUSOV:	Sophie, eh? That's all you see,
	You youngsters. Prettiness. Hm. I suppose
	She dropped a word or twitched her pretty nose
	Or something. Has you dangling on a rope,
	Already, eh?
CHATSKY:	Perhaps. Without much hope.
FAMUSOV:	"My dream come true," she says. That sort of hit,
	Eh? Got you started.
CHATSKY:	Not a bit of it.
FAMUSOV:	What was it now, that dream of hers? A lot
	Of rot, whatever it was.
CHATSKY:	I cling to what
	My own eyes tell me. What they tell me is
	She's going to lash susceptibilities.
FAMUSOV:	To hell with that. Back to realities.
	Some traveller's tales. Tell me where you've been
	Wandering all these years. I bet you've seen
	Some hot spots, so to speak.
CHATSKY:	*(agitated)* Can't tell you now,
	Except that I've not finished yet. Somehow
	The wandering fit's come back. The wide world's there,
	And I – I've hardly wandered anywhere.
	I came to say I'm back. I was in a hurry
	To see you. But my family will worry
	If they hear I'm here and haven't been home yet.

I'd better go. Back in an hour. Won't forget

The skimpiest details of my travels. You

Shall have it first and can recount it to

Whoever you wish.

He starts to leave, murmuring:

So pretty.

FAMUSOV: *(solus)*   Pretty weird,

This situation. First of all I feared

It might be that Molchalin. Dream come true.

Molchalin is my darlin'. That won't do.

Nor will this. A pauper. A gadabout,

Spendthrift, butterfly. I can't work out

What's best to do. O Lord in heaven, you oughta

Know what it means to have a grown-up daughter.

No, of course not. Not you. You've got a rather

Limited sense of being a good father.

Still, God help me.

CURTAIN

Act Two

Later that morning. The scene is the same. **FAMUSOV** *is seated,* **PETER** *his servant standing and attentive.*

FAMUSOV: Peter. Take down this. No, take down these.

The word's *take down*. Pass me the diary, please.

But why do I say "please" to one who's got

A hole in his elbow. Never mind. Now what

Do we start with? Yes. On Tuesday week

Dinner with Parasceva. A unique

Occasion. We're promised river trout.

Philosophy – you know that word? Without

Philosophy we're nothing. Here's the question:

Three hours of food, then three days indigestion.

How does philosophy cope with that, my lad?

Philosophise, and you go raving mad.

Philosophy is not bicarbonate

Of soda. Now then. Write – on the same date –

No, Thursday. That's the day of the funeral.

That makes one really philosophical.

Humanity, humanity – it's heterodox

To think you can avoid that wooden box,

Creeping to where you neither stand nor sit.

But – here's philosophy – accepting it

Is the only way to leave a name behind,

Permitting your posterity to find

A fine example of a life lived well,

Like this one. His encomia will tell

Of an honourable member of the Court,

A chamberlain, no less, the upright sort

Who passes all his honours to his son,

Just like his father. Oh, well done, well done.

Wealthy, he married wealthy. And his brood

And grandbrood too have piously pursued

The same example. They all married rich.

But now he's dead. Ah, Kuzma Petrovich,

Requiescat – that means R.I.P.

The men of Moscow – great. Greatness, you see,

Is something we inherit, not create.

Philosophy, my boy. And now the date

That follows – the same? – no, that can't be.

It must be Friday or Saturday. We

Go to a christening. Balance, balance, you see –

Death. Birth. The doctor's widow? It can't be she

That's had the baby, can it? Ought to be,

Though, by my reckoning. Still, it doesn't show.

Ah, Chatsky, good to see you.

For **CHATSKY** *has come in.*

CHATSKY: Busy?

FAMUSOV: Oh,

So so. Sit down. Right, Peter, off you go.

PETER *leaves.*

> Making notes, you know, of that and this,
>
> So many things – appointments. You can miss
>
> The trivial because of the essential.

CHATSKY: Are you all right?

> You seem, well, worried. You have the sort of tight
>
> Gut of a man who's holding something in,
>
> A grimace that impersonates a grin.
>
> It's not perhaps your daughter, Sophie, is it?
>
> Is she well, ill? It's an inopportune visit?
>
> If so, I'll go. You're clearly a worried man.

FAMUSOV: Not worried. Serious. At my age can

> You expect to find me squatting, kicking out,
>
> Doing a Russian dance like some peasant lout?

CHATSKY: I'm not here to award a dancing trophy.

> I merely asked about your daughter Sophie.
>
> Is she all right?

FAMUSOV: Is she all right? All wrong,

> You singing first one song then another song –
>
> *There's no one in the world like Sophie.* Then:
>
> *Is she all right?* Then you go back again
>
> To *No one in the world like.* Tell me straight,
>
> A yes or no, and don't prevaricate.
>
> You like the girl? You've travelled, and you've been
>
> All the world over, but you've never seen

A girl like Sophie. What are you getting at –
Marriage?

CHATSKY: Why do you ask?

FAMUSOV: Well, as for that,
I'm a sort of relative. And one who's rather
Closer than most. They tell me I'm her father.

CHATSKY: What would you say then if I answered yes? –
Meaning I want your *yes* and hers.

FAMUSOV: I'd guess
You don't know your own mind. You may have travelled,
But otherwise you're a ball of wool. Unravelled.
I say, that's good. You do nothing. You're not
An officer in anything. No spot
In the administration. Steel your nerve,
Man, join the services.

CHATSKY: I'd willingly serve.
It's the servility that makes me vomit.

FAMUSOV: There you go. You won't get a damned thing from it,
This cocksure cockiness. You youngsters need
To learn from past success how to succeed.
Learn from your forebears, or else learn from me,
Learn from my uncle Max. He'd never be
Seen eating his scoff or swilling his tea
From china. Silver? No, gold was his platter.
He'd think that something was the blasted matter

If he'd less than a hundred at his call and beck –

Servants, you know, not serfs. He'd wring the neck

Of any serf he saw picking his nose.

And how many do you think he had of those?

He couldn't count. Whenever he went out,

There was the coach and six. A big man. Stout,

But it was the medals weighed him down. His sort

Was nurtured in the old imperial court –

God forgive her sins – Katy the Great.

There she was circled round by men of weight,

Two ton apiece. They wouldn't even nod

When people bowed at them. They'd nod at God,

Perhaps – that was his due. They ate ambrosia

And drank that other stuff. They'd suffer nausea

At anything else. And there was Uncle Max,

A damned big knout for disobedient backs,

Haughty as hell, nose like a blunderbuss,

But when he'd got to be obsequious –

You know that word? – he could bend over double.

One day he thought he was in damned big trouble.

A morning levee, it was. The old man fell –

He'd tripped on something – fell, it hurt like hell.

He nearly cracked his occiput in half.

What does Her Majesty do? She starts to laugh.

What does *he* do? Gets up, and falls again.

On purpose, see. The laugh goes on. And then

He does it once more. She'd have laughed for ever

If there'd been time. Clever, eh? That was clever.

He fell and rose. Rose like the morning sun

But more than once a day. God, he got on.

My uncle Max. By God, he earned respect –

Royal whist parties, balls. There he is, decked

With medals. Always the centre of attention.

You want promotion? You require a pension?

You want exemption from a property tax?

A prince for a son-in-law? Ask Uncle Max.

You, you modern puppies. Get away.

CHATSKY: All right, all right – it may be as you say.

The world's gone soft. Because it no longer suits

This generation to go licking boots

And arses to have sinecures and honours

And cast-iron penny medals showered upon us.

There was no choice then. Lose your head in war,

In peacetime let it bump along the floor.

As for the poor – you rub theirs in the dirt.

Weave flattery like lace for the royal shirt,

And turn God's truth into political error.

That was the age of grovelling and terror,

Disguised as zeal to serve the swine on top.

You think that Russia changes? No. Full stop.

We won't disturb your uncle's rotting carcass.

It's ghastly, probing that primeval dark, as

Paupers grope in garbage, to recall

How some would give worlds for the chance to fall

To raise a royal laugh. Christ, what ambition.

There are still plenty with that disposition.

But now a whiff of shame sweetens the air.

We thumb our noses at the pigs up there.

FAMUSOV: Oh God, he's a subversive.

CHATSKY: A wind's blowing.

There's air to breathe. We know now where we're going.

We prick the shibboleths like toy balloons,

Don't rush to join the regiment of buffoons.

FAMUSOV: Oh, my God —

CHATSKY: Kicking our heels in anterooms,

Fetching chairs, sick of the sick perfumes

Of haughty patronesses — seen, not heard,

Cackling at a pseudo-witty word

Filched from some poet left to rot in jail.

FAMUSOV: You're preaching liberty, you know.

CHATSKY: I fail

To see why I shouldn't. The real people are

Those who think a little and live far

From metropolitan corruption, people who

Do the work they know they have to do

For the work's sake, not the disdainful others.

FAMUSOV: Soon you'll be saying all men should be brothers.

That's blasphemy. I wouldn't have such people

Visible even from a Kremlin steeple.

Authority. You jeer at it.

CHATSKY: All right,

I've said enough for the moment.

FAMUSOV: This is quite

Unendurable. This is –

CHATSKY: Since I show

No mercy to your generation, blow

Down mine. I won't blubber if you do.

FAMUSOV: I do not know you, sir. You're vicious. You

Had better say no more.

CHATSKY: I say no more,

Not for the moment.

FAMUSOV: My poor ears are sore

With all that poison.

CHATSKY: Well, I've corked the bottle.

FAMUSOV: These youngsters – blasphemy. God in heaven, what'll

They do when they take over?

CHATSKY: You can scrub

It all from the record.

A **SERVANT** *stands at the door.*

SERVANT: Colonel Skalozub.

41

FAMUSOV:	You'll be had up. Shoved up against a wall,
	Shot.
CHATSKY:	It seems that someone's come to call.
FAMUSOV:	But first you'll hear the thunder at the door
	Of the state police. At night.
CHATSKY:	As I said before,
	You have a caller.
FAMUSOV:	Mutiny's abroad.
	Chaos and anarchy. O my dear Lord,
	Hell's breaking loose.
SERVANT:	It's Colonel Skalozub.
	Shall I show him up, sir?
FAMUSOV:	Satan, Beelzebub
	Lurk in the alleyways. Yes, you benighted
	Idiot, say please come in. Say delighted.
	Off with you.

The SERVANT *goes out.*

As for you, mind what you say.
You don't meet men like this one every day.
He's big, important. Medals by the ton.
Wealthy, so he was destined to get on.
Early promotion. He'll be a general soon.
Don't play the revolutionary buffoon
With him. I know it was only your little game.
It was naughty, wasn't it? But just the same,

Don't joke. It's quite an honour, such as he

Paying me a visit. You know me.

I like visits as much as any man alive,

But here in Moscow two and two make five.

In other words, he's after little Sophie.

He's got his medals. Here's another trophy,

Or so he thinks. Nonsense. I'm wise to it.

I'll let him nibble round the edge a bit.

Her marriage isn't an immediate worry.

She's young. Neither of us is in a hurry.

But still – God disposes. So please don't swear

That black is white while he is sitting there.

Do drop these cranky notions. Where is he?

Shown to the other room? I'll go and see.

He does. **CHATSKY** *is left alone.*

CHATSKY: Fuss and hurry. Sophie – engaged? That's why

They treat me like a nobody. Not that I

Care much. But why is she not here? This colonel –

Her father seems to care a right infernal

Lot about him. Perhaps he's not alone

In that. I suppose the fault's my own,

Going away for three years –

FAMUSOV *leads the colonel in.*

FAMUSOV: Come this way,

Dear colonel. Brrrr. By God, it's a cold day.

You must be frozen. Let me get you warm.

I'll open up the stove.

SKALOZUB: That's dashed bad form.

You're a gentleman if not an officer.

Gentlemen shouldn't do that.

FAMUSOV: My dear sir,

I'll do anything for my friends. You're aware of that.

Undo your sword. Sit down. Give me your hat.

SKALOZUB: *You* sit down. Your standing gets on my nerves.

FAMUSOV: Certainly.

They all sit, CHATSKY *at some distance from the others, like a pariah.*

And now – your friend deserves

A little more than friendship. Did you know

That we're related? Distant, of course. And so

No claim on family property. A surprise?

For me too. It was your cousin put me wise

Only the other day. She's now in heaven, a

Sort of saint – Anastasia Nikolayevna –

She is the link between us.

SKALOZUB: Sorry, sir.

I wouldn't know. I never served with her.

FAMUSOV: Oh, come come – share my pleasure. When I find

Kinship, I'm ecstatically inclined.

I trace it to the ocean's bed or deeper.

You know the saying – Am I my brother's keeper?

Well, I'm my cousins', also nephews', nieces'.

The department that I run would fall to pieces

If I didn't have my sister's children in it.

Sister-in-law's as well. When I get a minute,

Sent from on high, about a decoration

Or small promotion, I think of a relation.

You've got to look after your kith and kin.

Molchalin's different. I put Molchalin in

His secretarial post because he's good.

Now, to shift back to your neighbourhood

– My friend your cousin. He made it amply clear

You gave him lots of help with his career.

SKALOZUB: We got citations in the self-same year.

Thirtieth Chasseurs.

FAMUSOV: Happy the man with such

A son, eh? Wasn't there a ribbon with a touch

Of something pretty dangling at the bottom?

SKALUZOB: He got a medal. Not too many got 'em.

Not many stuck it out so long at base.

Survived. We both survived. That's no disgrace.

I got a thing to hang around my neck.

FAMUSOV: You're right. When there's the prospect of a wreck,

It doesn't do to stick it out on deck.

A charming man, your cousin.

SKALOZUB: Used to be,

Until he started thinking. Damn it, he

Was due for promotion, but he slung his hook,

Went to the country, even read a book.

FAMUSOV: Youth, youth. It's terrible, all this reading.

And yet he had you as a model, leading

The manly life. You were made colonel when?

SKALOZUB: I was lucky. When a lot of the senior men

Got shot.

FAMUSOV: The Lord looketh after his own.

SKALOZUB: That's in the Bible, is it? Some I've known

Have had better luck. Look at our brigadier.

FAMUSOV: Luck indeed. That should be you.

SKALOZUB: A mere

Toss of the coin, you know. I'm quite content.

But it took two years to get a regiment.

FAMUSOV: And soon it'll be a division, eh? Such talent,

Such rich rewards await the brave and gallant.

Such happiness too for – er – the general's lady.

SKALUZOB: It's an idea. When a man makes the grade, he

Wants to sort of pass the glory on.

FAMUSOV: Very well put. No son – the glory's gone.

Plenty of daughters, sisters, nieces, cousins,

Brides – why, you can count them in their dozens.

No shortage here in Moscow. A fresh batch

Here every year. This city has no match

For brides. But you have to stay here. Make your catch

On the spot. Not moon over statistics.

SKALOZUB: True. Distance poses problems of logistics.

FAMUSOV: Moscow has perfect taste and perfect style.

And perfect rules of conduct, too. Why, I'll

Wager there's no better custom than the one

That passes honours to the eldest son.

A man may not be much, but if he rates

Two thousand souls on family estates,

He'll find a bride and a damned good one too.

It's being what you are, not what you do.

Somebody may be smart, full of himself,

But he's shoved on the matrimonial shelf.

Cleverness doesn't pay. Whatever they say,

It's birth that counts, and that's the Moscow way.

And may I mention something else that counts,

Dear sir, near-cousin, something amounts

To Christian virtue? – Hospitality.

Anyone's welcome here. Say dinner. We

Can always add another fork and knife.

Let the world come, the whole world and its wife –

They're welcome, within reason. Another matter,

While we're on Moscow virtues. Though they chatter,

The young, I mean, the devils speak their mind.

Rank heresy sometimes. But at the end you find

It's really the good old ways that they'll be praising.

Such energy. It isn't hell they're raising –

Storms in a teacup. Talking about those –

Teacups, cards, the ladies, do you suppose

That when their parties foam into a riot

It's because they haven't sense to keep things quiet?

I know women. I was married once.

Harness their energy. See the response

Of Moscow if you shoved them in the Senate.

Make them drill the troops, that's it. But when it

Comes to breeding daughters – the pride of Russia.

We had a visit from the King of Prussia –

He was astounded by the sheer assortment

Of Moscow beauty. Not looks perhaps – deportment,

Education, dress, facial grimaces.

They don't need words when they have got such faces.

They'll sing French songs and belt out the top notes.

And as for love – every one of them dotes

On military men. They're patriotic,

That's what they are. You know, it's idiotic

To buzz around the world. It's a dead loss – go

Where you will, there's no place quite like Moscow.

SKALOZUB: That fire you had improved the place a bit.

FAMUSOV: Incendiarists. Don't let me think of it.

              Painful. Well, yes, in a sense that's true –

New streets, new houses. Even the Kremlin's new.

CHATSKY: New streets, new houses – see them and enjoy.

Old prejudice? Too precious to destroy.

FAMUSOV: Look here, you. Didn't I tell you to keep quiet? He

Doesn't have much patriotic piety.

Sorry – Chatsky – Andrew Chatsky's son.

Not in the Service. Could be, though. He's one

Of those who will not use the brains God gave him.

Writer, translator – wasted, heaven save him,

A pity.

CHATSKY: Keep your pity, praise as well.

Your praise appals me.

FAMUSOV: All right, why do you sell

Poems to papers if you don't want praise?

The critics praise you, don't they?

CHATSKY: Please don't raise

Those tatty phantoms of an age long gone,

In love with Tsarist dungeons, battening on

Ideas that were exploded years ago,

Losing their teeth and reason. Oh, hallo,

Peter the Great is dead. They grumble, fumble,

Play the same tune. And where they tread they stumble,

The old, our national fathers, with their ample

Paunches and prejudices. They set an example

To us? Raising their palaces, dropping stones

On the great plenitude of paupers' bones,
Gorging and bidding others gorge, they squelch
In turtle soup, on sturgeon's eggs, and belch
Their praises to the great lord god of guzzling.
Their enemy is thought, a dog for muzzling.
The gambling rouйs, protected by a mob
Of smirking servants, always ripe to rob
The bastards blind. Dead drunk and laying out
Their vomit. Waking crapulous to shout
For whores or catamites. Snatching from mothers
Whole wagonloads of infant serfs. Bare brothers
And barer sisters forced to copulate
To entertain the great men of the state.
A nation that spreads gold paint on its knavery
And prides itself on being built on slavery.
These are the swine that we have to respect,
Honour their brainlessness, while we neglect
The shivering geniuses. Isn't penal Siberia
A frozen monument to the superior?
When a young man's too honourable to tout
For jobs, or butter up a loathsome lout
For grease and fever, one who's set his heart
On gaining wisdom, practising an art,
Seeking out truth and beauty – that's absurd, a
Mob of gentlemen cries fire, thieves, murder.

The man's a dreamer. Dreams! The state's in danger.

Smother him. Kill him. He's a dog with mange, a

Leper, foul, infectious. Put him down.

He's strutting naked through the well-dressed town.

Dress – that's not just a thing to keep them warm.

Dress has a message. If it's uniform,

The message is: Worship us, we're the peak,

Untouchable, incomparable, unique.

Look how the wives and daughters dote on it.

I know its damned attraction. The bug bit

Me once as a boy. The time the Royal Guard

Rivalled the sunlight in the Palace yard.

The Guards. The women near pulled down their drawers

To demonstrate that wars go well with whores.

FAMUSOV: He'll drop me in the soup, by God –

A **SERVANT** *has entered.*

SERVANT: Please, sir –

A messenger from the Under Minister.

FAMUSOV: Colonel, I'll be in my study.

He follows the **SERVANT** *out.*

SKALOZUB: Rather good,

That. The Guards, eh? Pets of the people. Would

They pull their knickers down for the First Army?

It's the gold braid that does it. They alarm me

Toy soldiers, eh? A finer body of men,

Our lot. Slim-waisted, upright. Now and then

We get a man with foreign languages.

SOPHIE *and* **LIZA** *run in.*

SOPHIE: My God, he's fallen. I daren't look. God, he's

Killed.

She faints.

CHATSKY: Who?

SKALOZUB: Who's killed?

CHATSKY: ...She's dead with fright.

SKALOZUB: What's going on? Who's dead?

CHATSKY: She'll be all right.

What about him, though?

SKALOZUB: The old man's had a tumble?

LIZA: Fate, sir. When fate strikes, who is to grumble?

Mr Molchalin went to mount a horse.

He'd got his foot in the stirrup. Then the force

Of the horse rearing made him sort of fall

Smack on his skull.

SKALOZUB: On his head? That all?

Pulled on the reins, eh? Damned bad horsemanship.

I'll go and see the damage.

CHATSKY: Here. A sip

Of water's what she needs. Sprinkle. Don't stop.

Loosen her laces. Drink another drop.

And try and little smear of vinegar

Upon her temples. She's breathing easier.

Got a fan?

LIZA: Here.

She fans. The COLONEL *has gone out.* CHATSKY *looks out of the window.*

CHATSKY: He's on his feet already,

Molchalin. Walking. But a bit unsteady.

She got upset for nothing.

LIZA: Sensitive. She

Can't stand by and watch when somebody

Falls down head first.

CHATSKY: Go on. A little more

Water. Sprinkle. Gently.

SOPHIE: Who's here? For

A moment I thought it was – thought it was – How is he?

CHATSKY: All right, but it would be all the same to me

If he broke his neck.

SOPHIE: Cold-blooded murderer.

Out of my sight.

CHATSKY: Of course you'd much prefer

For me to be a hypocrite. That's splendid.

SOPHIE: Run to him. Help him.

CHATSKY: And leave you unattended?

Ah, no.

SOPHIE: What does it matter about me?

You laugh at people's troubles. Yes, you'd be

Laughing your head off if they killed your father.

Come on, hurry, Liza.

LIZA: No need to bother.

He's all right, see.

CHATSKY: She's flustered, in a spin –

That only means one thing.

SOPHIE: They're coming in.

Oh, he can't lift his arm. His poor poor arm.

CHATSKY: I wouldn't mind dying like that.

SKALOZUB *comes in with* **MOLCHALIN**, *whose arm is bound with a handkerchief.*

SKALOZUB: A false alarm.

Bit of a bruise, that's all.

MOLCHALIN: I apologise.

I must have frightened you.

SKALOZUB: Why, damn your eyes,

A lot of fuss for nothing.

SOPHIE: *(calmly)* Not serious?

Yet I'm still shaking.

CHATSKY: (Not a lot of fuss

For him now. That's strange.)

SOPHIE: You know, I'm brave

When there's an accident or a close shave

That just involves myself. Like on the road.

The carriage overturns. I'm cool.

CHATSKY: (As a toad.)

SOPHIE:	Put it back upright. Off we go galloping.
	But other people – the least little thing
	Upsets me. Even people I don't know.
	It's the way I'm made. I just can't help it.

CHATSKY: (So

She wants him to excuse her for once feeling
Sorry for someone. Somewhat unappealing.)

SKALOZUB: A little story. The Princess Lasova,

A widow, you know, is one of those ladies who are
Fond of riding, but without a proper
Companion. Well, last week she came a cropper.
Her groom had dozed off. Now she's a rib shorter
And is looking for a husband to support her.
It's different in the Bible, eh? It was Adam
Who lost a rib so he could get a madam,
Eh, eh?

SOPHIE: You, sir, where's your generosity?

You're always talking, aren't you, with pomposity,
Of the brotherhood of man.

CHATSKY: Of woman, too.

Siblinghood call it. Well, madame, with you
I was solicitous enough, I thought – a
Loosening of the stays, a splash of water.
But for whose benefit I'm not quite sure.

He leaves brusquely.

SOPHIE:	Well, it's all over now. Oh, Colonel, you're
	Coming to us this evening?
SKALOZUB:	Early?
SOPHIE:	–Ish.
	A few friends of the family. And a dish
	Of tea. Some dancing to the pianoforte.
SKALOZUB:	I'll come. But where's your father gone? I thought he
	Had something to discuss. Excuse me. I
	Will just look in on him. Goodbye.
SOPHIE:	Goodbye.
	Mr Molchalin, sir, you ought to know
	Your life is precious to me. Why do you go
	Putting yourself in danger? Such a relief
	To know you're not in pain.
MOLCHALIN:	No groans, no grief,
	I tied it up, see, with my handkerchief.
LIZA:	Nothing at all, just like I went and told yer.
	He wants to act the little wounded soldier.
	But there's going to be something serious, I can tell,
	After that fainting fit. You know, you fell
	Into his clutches – Mr Chatsky's. He
	Is going to have some fun. He'll tell them: "She
	Fell pretty heavily for Whatisname."
	And then there's the colonel. Ah, they're all the same,
	These days. The men, the ladies. Everyone chatters.

56

SOPHIE:	Why should you think that I should think it matters?
	I'll love if I wish and say so, so that's that, as
	Bright as daylight and as clear as paint.
	It was my heart that ordered me to faint,
	But otherwise I think I showed restraint,
	Didn't I? Didn't speak, didn't betray
	My feelings. Didn't even look your way.
MOLCHALIN:	Well, to be honest, you were pretty frank.
SOPHIE:	But, as for that, you have my love to thank.
	When I saw you lying there I could have hurled
	Myself out after you. The whole wide world –
	What do I care how it can scold and scoff?
MOLCHALIN:	I hope this kind of candour won't rub off
	On me.
SOPHIE:	You're frightened of a duel?
MOLCHALIN:	Well,
	Tongues can hit worse than guns. And, truth to tell,
	It makes my situation shaky.
LIZA:	Spare
	Us the details. Miss Sophie, go in there,
	Tell them, and make a sort of joke of it,
	About your having this queer fainting fit,
	Thinking it was your dad that cut his loaf,
	And if you see that Chatsky give the oaf
	A smirk or two and talk about old times.

	Put them off the scent. The only crime's
	Telling the truth these days. Men are so dense
	They hate the truth and get fat on pretence.
MOLCHALIN:	I won't presume to offer you advice.
SOPHIE:	You want me to go, though – play at being nice,
	Swallow my feelings, act agreeable,
	If I've the strength. One of these days I'll kill
	Dear Chatsky.

She goes off. **MOLCHALIN**'s *tone changes very rapidly.*

MOLCHALIN:	Clever, aren't you? Full of fun,
	Lively. Give us a kiss. A peck. Come on.
LIZA:	Let me go. You've got her, you don't need me.
MOLCHALIN:	Like calls to like. She's not my class, not she.
	I love you.
LIZA:	You love her.
MOLCHALIN:	You little beauty,
	You know that it's a matter of my duty
	To getting on in life. But you, your big
	Brown eyes, your this and that –
LIZA:	Paws off, you pig.
	I'm for when you're bored with gentility,
	Isn't that it?
MOLCHALIN:	No, it's not. Listen to me,
	I've got some spiffing presents for you – a kid-
	Skin dressing-case with mirrors in the lid,

All gilt and openwork. A mother-of-pearl

Toilet set to please my little girl,

A pin cushion with decorative beads,

A needle case set round with kind of seeds

Of little pearls – real – and a pair of scissors.

Creams and lip salves (come on, give us a kiss) as

Well as scent – jasmine and mignonette.

LIZA: Presents won't get you what you think you'll get.

You'd better tell me why you're so afraid

To speak out to the mistress, not the maid.

MOLCHALIN: *(drooping)* I'm not at all the thing. I think that I'll

Lie down a bit. Do come and stay awhile

After dinner. I've lots of things to say.

SOPHIE *comes in. He recomposes his countenance. He goes, looking ill.*

SOPHIE: Nobody there. Everyone's gone away.

I'm not at all the thing. I don't want dinner.

You'd better see Mr Molchalin in a

Little while and tell him to come to me.

She goes off in the opposite direction to **MOLCHALIN.** **LIZA** *is alone.*

LIZA: Lord have mercy. Why do there have to be

People. People. People. Let me die.

She's after him. He's after me. And I – ?

I seem to be the only one who's frightened

Of love. May heaven bless the unenlightened.

Love – it's all shrieking, shifting, shocking, shoving.

God may be love, but God love the unloving.

CURTAIN

Act Three

Scene One

The Same. Afternoon. **CHATSKY** *is alone.*

CHATSKY: She has to tell me, has to tell me who –

Which one of the intolerable two?

Molchalin, archetypal bloody fool,

Seems to have cracked the sempiternal rule

– Unredeemable unintelligence

Is stuck in a perpetual present tense

And can't break free from its decreed cocoon.

As for that growling grumbling great bassoon,

Half-throttled by his collar, Skalozub,

Whose brain is just an etiolated grub

In an unedible apple, stuck in a groove as

Muddy as his own inept manoeuvres,

One of the ruling class of soldier-shirkers

Whose talent is for waltzes and mazurkas –

What can I say? All I can say's enough!

Love has to be a game of blind man's buff.

While I –

SOPHIE *comes in.*

You're here. Alone. At last. Just what
I wanted.

SOPHIE: (What you wanted. And I not.)

CHATSKY:	It wasn't me you came to look for?
SOPHIE:	No.
CHATSKY:	Don't be too sure. Well, still, you're here. Although
	I know it's an awkward question, I must ask it.
	Who is it that you love?
SOPHIE:	The world's a basket
	Of variegated flowers. And I love flowers.
CHATSKY:	Cryptic. And in this lovable world of ours
	Do you have preferences?
SOPHIE:	I love my family.
CHATSKY:	The fingers of rejection touch me – clammily.
	Shall I buy a yard of rope, have misspent youth
	Nipped in the bud?
SOPHIE:	Do you want to know the truth?
	I'll put it in a nutshell. King of criticism,
	Lord of the foul crack and the wounding witticism,
	That's you. Judging the world, a sort of God,
	Blind to the normal, sneering at the odd,
	You are the odd one out.
CHATSKY:	I am? You mean that?
SOPHIE:	You're fond of mirrors. Strange you haven't seen that
	Destructive eye. Strange that you haven't heard
	The swish of swords in every little word.
	You laugh – what an eccentric world it is!
	But you're the prince of eccentricities.

CHATSKY:	Not of egregious stupidities,
	I like to think. Molchalin, for example.
SOPHIE:	I'm not surprised. So – add him to your ample
	Collection. You're crammed with spite, and you're not showing
	A single break in the blackness. Thanks. I'm going.

But **CHATSKY** *holds her back.*

CHATSKY:	(Pretences, foul pretences – just this once.)
	Listen. Molchalin used to be a dunce,
	But I can see he's quite transformed – a miracle,
	Really. And my aiming a satirical
	Shaft or two at him – now – is out of place.
	I can see that. I sort of turned my face
	Against the man's capacity for change.
	Change, after all, is not so very strange.
	Change, someone said, is evidence of life.
	Molchalin – fine, his wit is like a knife,
	His intelligence is sunlight. But does he
	Have fire, have passion, sensibility,
	A heart that thuds with love and leaves him breathless,
	A high frustrated urge to set down deathless
	Sonnets and odes to celebrate your grace,
	Your beauty, the enchantment of your face?
	Believe me – ah, that transcendental urge is
	Certainly here, in me, it seethes and surges,
	Rages, wages war with gelid reason.

But he? He's meek, he's tongue-tied, gentle, he's an

Undercooked cutlet out of heaven's oven.

Sorry. I mean that, out of perverted love, an

Urge to make its object better than

It really is, you have re-made the man

In your own heart. You've fashioned him a mask

He doesn't know he's wearing. Christian meekness,

Saintly forbearance – those can be glossed as weakness,

Bloodlessness. All right. I only ask

If he is good enough for you. Think of it,

Scrape off the pigments from your exquisite

Creation. Look. And see what's really there.

And if you're really sure – I'll go somewhere

Where amorous madness can be cooled to sanity,

I can amuse myself with some inanity

Or other, and grow cold, forgetful of

That bad time when I used to be in love.

SOPHIE: (I never meant to get him in this state.)

You over- or else under-estimate

Quite simple things. Like Mr Molchalin's arm.

I really thought he'd broken it. What harm

If I reacted in the way I did?

I find it hard to clamp a saucepan lid

On overboiling sensitivity.

It doesn't matter who it is, you see.

Anyone who's in trouble. You're different,

You're just the opposite. You laugh, you vent

Your scorn. I mention him, and then you poke

Fun. Joke after joke after joke after joke.

CHATSKY: There are other objects in my life than laughter.

I'm drunk with it, you think. The morning after

I know it's bores that are my enemies.

SOPHIE: Get to know him better. You'll see there is

Nothing boring there.

CHATSKY: *(with heat)* Perhaps you'd tell

How you got to know this unboring one so well.

SOPHIE: I didn't try to. God brought us together.

God's bound the household in a friendly tether,

Thanks to his niceness. He's been here three years

Working for Papa. Papa can call forth tears

With his unreasonable anger sometimes, but

Mr Molchalin smiles, keeps his mouth shut,

Rebukes with silence, then disarms with such

A sweet look of forgiveness. Ah, he's much

Too good for this bad world. When he has leisure,

He doesn't go in for laughs or boyish pleasure.

He plays cards with the old folk.

CHATSKY: He plays cards

With the old folk. Good.

SOPHIE: Yes, good. As regards

Things like showing off with cruel wit,

Well, he's not got the temperament for it.

And firing off a cynical *barrage*

Is not the way to build a good *ménage.*

CHATSKY: (She doesn't really give a damn for him.)

SOPHIE: He smiles when all the world is looking grim.

He's modest, quiet, calm and deferential,

He keeps his eyes down, so that the essential

Goodness isn't a rebuke to anyone.

I love him. There. I've said it.

CHATSKY: Oh, well done.

And how about the other brilliant claimant –

That cerebral nullity in army raiment,

Whose soldierly achievements add to zero,

But, since he says so, has to be a hero?

Skalozub –

SOPHIE: Not a hero in my book.

LIZA *comes in. She whispers.*

LIZA: Mr Molchalin, Miss, has come to look

For you.

SOPHIE: Forgive me, please, I have to hurry.

CHATSKY: Where to?

SOPHIE: My hairdresser.

CHATSKY: You mustn't worry.

To gild that crinal glory is absurd.

SOPHIE: His curlers will get cold.

She leaves, or starts to.

CHATSKY: Cold is the word.

SOPHIE: *(before going into her room)*

We're expecting people for a party.

CHATSKY: Wait!

Can't I come in as well and celebrate

The pleasure that I had there, breathe the air

That's dissipated and gone God knows where,

Warm myself, revive myself by feeling

I was a part of it – under that ceiling,

On that carpet – I promise I won't stay

Too long. I'll drink it in then go away

And drink a measure at the English Club,

Pray for the soul of Colonel Skalozub,

And for the mind of Molchalin –

But **SOPHIE** *and* **LIZA** *go on in, loudly locking the door.*

So it's he –

Incredible – Still, if he has to be

Her husband, a debilitous intellection

Doesn't mean weakness in the main direction.

He can beget nice offspring, I should think –

Pink cheeks, thoughts, and opinions. Everything pink.

There is the man, tiptoeing in, so quiet.

How did he get her heart to rave and riot?

Hallo, Molchalin, let's have a word or two.

I haven't had a chance to speak with you.

How's life?

MOLCHALIN: My life, sir? Same as it always is.

CHATSKY: Crammed with the usual banalities?

MOLCHALIN: Day after day, today like yesterday.

CHATSKY: A lot of work, and then a little play –

Desk to card table – that's the pattern, eh?

At the appointed hours of ebb and flow.

MOLCHALIN: Oh, since I was moved up to Archives, you know,

My efforts and my energy, if so

I may describe them, won me three bonuses.

CHATSKY: Honour and social rank – that duo is

Attractive to you?

MOLCHALIN: Sir, I'm unpretentious.

I'm economical and conscientious,

And hope, sir, that those gifts will be rewarded.

CHATSKY: Fine gifts. Better than any I recorded.

MOLCHALIN: You were passed over, weren't you? Did you blot

Your copybook?

CHATSKY: ... Did I blot my what?

Never mind. A human being makes

Promotion lists, and humans make mistakes.

MOLCHALIN: We were surprised.

CHATSKY: What for?

MOLCHALIN:	Hearts used to bleed
	For you, forgive the metaphor.
CHATSKY:	No need.
MOLCHALIN:	Tatióna Yъrevna told us all about it
	After she'd been to Petersburg. No doubt, it
	Was something to do with something – a fall from grace?
	Is that the expression? Said something to his face
	That didn't go well – the Chief Minister –
CHATSKY:	And what the hell had it to do with her?
MOLCHALIN:	Tatióna Yъrevna?
CHATSKY:	We're not acquainted.
MOLCHALIN:	Tatióna Yъrevna!!
CHATSKY:	An over-painted
	Lady whose brain is said to be rather sketchy.
MOLCHALIN:	Tatióna Yъrevna!!! You forget – she
	Has relatives in the highest echelon –
	All departmental heads. I could go on.
	But it's enough to say she's influential.
	Pay her a call. Be like me – deferential.
CHATSKY:	My calls on ladies are of a different kind.
MOLCHALIN:	So affable, so helpful, and you'll find
	She's generous to a frightening extent.
	She holds these balls – from Christmas up till Lent,
	And garden parties at her summer villa.
	Beg her to fix you (and I'm sure she will) a

Post in Moscow, a nice easy one,

You'll get some bonuses and have some fun.

CHATSKY: Thanks. When I work, I work. And when I fool,

I fool. I'm not an alumnus of that school

Of clever devils who combine the two.

MOLCHALIN: Why should that be a crime? Why, some day you

Could be like Tom Fomнch, a section head

Under three ministers. You must have read

The things he's written. Now he's been transferred

Here.

CHATSKY: He has the brains of a stuffed bird,

The stuff he writes is horse's excrement.

MOLCHALIN: You can't have read him.

CHATSKY: Read one thing, then went

To use it, with a minimal compunction,

In the discharging of a natural function.

MOLCHALIN: Really! Me, I find him stylish – very –

But then I don't claim to be literary.

CHATSKY: No need to tell me that.

MOLCHALIN: A man like me

Shouldn't presume to have opinions.

CHATSKY: We

Are not children, men, and, God be thanked,

Not bound by law to see the sacrosanct

In other men's opinions.

MOLCHALIN:	Oh no, no,
	We juniors must be careful how we go.
	When I've got seniority, the case
	Will certainly be altered.

CHATSKY: (God, that face

Matches the inner vacuousness. Invoking

The god of love for *that*? She must be joking!)

CURTAIN

Scene Two

All the doors of the drawing room, except that leading to SOPHIE's *bedchamber, have been flung open, revealing a number of brightly lighted reception areas. Servants are busily at work.*

HEAD SERVANT: Serge, Ivan – to work, cut out the talk.

Cards, card tables, billiard cues and chalk.

He knocks on SOPHIE's *door.*

Liza, Elizabeth – tell your mistress we're

Just about ready. Mrs Gorich is here

With her husband. And there's another carriage – no, two –

Just arriving.

The servants bustle off. CHATSKY *is revealed, alone.* NATHALIE GORICH, *a young married lady, glides in.*

NATHALIE: Am I mistaken? You,

Mr Chatsky?

CHATSKY: You're inspecting me

Like a museum exhibit. Have those three

Years changed me such a lot?

NATHALIE: I was sure

That you were miles from Moscow. Well, well. You're

Newly arrived?

CHATSKY: Newly.

NATHALIE: And staying here?

CHATSKY: That depends. You're plumper than you were,

Prettier too. All fire and rose. Fun

In your features. Something or someone

Seems to have made you younger.

NATHALIE: Well, I'm married.

CHATSKY: You never said. Or else the news miscarried.

NATHALIE: My husband's coming now. He's such a dear.

So loving. And such talent, though I fear

It's wasted. You're sure to love him.

CHATSKY: Well, I must

If he's your husband.

NATHALIE: Oh no, not for just

That reason. For what he is. My darling Plato.

Named for the Greek philosopher. His way to

Promotion – he's a soldier – a sad story –

They say he would have reached the final glory

Of military commander of this city –

But – well, he was retired. It's such a pity.

PLATO GORICH *comes in.*

This is my Plato.

CHATSKY: How are you, old son?

PLATO: Chatsky, dear boy!

CHATSKY: Known him for years. Well done.
A stunning victory.

PLATO: Her, you mean? Ah, yes.
Here I am. Matrimonial blessedness.
Retired to Moscow now, old boy.

CHATSKY: The tussle
For medals and promotion, the brisk bustle
Of life in camp, friends, comrades, all forgotten?
Quietly slacking, eh?

PLATO: Well, no, I've got an
Occupation. Studying the flute.
A thing by Albinoni –

CHATSKY: Didn't you toot
That opus all of five long years ago?

PLATO: One becomes kind of rigid. Marriage, you know.
When *you* get spliced, after the honeymoon,
You'll spend all day whistling the same old tune.
Boredom, you know.

CHATSKY: Old boy, don't tell me you
Get bored.

NATHALIE: There's lots of things he likes to do –
The riding school, the military review,

	Tattoo – Poor Plato, he can't do them now.
	He gets a little gloomy.
CHATSKY:	My dear chap, how
	Did this come about? Join up again. I'll wager
	You'll get a squadron, keep your rank of major.
NATHALIE:	His health's not good, you know.
CHATSKY:	Bad health? Since when?
NATHALIE:	He gets these awful headaches now and then,
	And rheumatism too.
CHATSKY:	Brisk exercise –
	That's what he needs. Riding. It would be wise
	To get a country residence.
NATHALIE:	My Plato
	Likes Moscow. Why, he'd be a mere potato
	If he had to vegetate, as some do.
CHATSKY:	Incredible. It's what they term a rum do.
	Remember the old life?
PLATO:	How could I forget,
	Dear boy? But things have changed.
NATHALIE:	Come on, my pet.
	You're standing in a draught. Your coat's undone.
	Do up your buttons.
PLATO:	Yes, my love.
NATHALIE:	Come on,
	Stand back from that door.

PLATO:	Old boy, as you can see,
	I'm not the man I was.
NATHALIE:	Come, follow me,
	Angel, we'll find somewhere a little warmer.
PLATO:	Yes, darling.
CHATSKY:	Yes, a shadow of your former
	Self. Dawn, boot and saddle, snorting stallion,
	Into the wind – the pride of the battalion.
	The autumn gales could slice you like a knife
	And you'd not worry –
PLATO:	It was a splendid life,
	Old boy.
NATHALIE:	Plato, come on.
CHATSKY:	I want a wife?

The **PRINCE** *and* **PRINCESS TUGO-UKHOVSKY** *come in with their six daughters.*

NATHALIE:	Prince Tugo-Ukhovsky! Dear Princess! I see
	Princess Zizi! And sweet Princess Mimi!

There is hearty kissing. Then everyone sits down and examines very closely the dress of the others.

PRINCESS 1:	Oh, what a pretty style.
PRINCESS 2:	Such pretty pleats.
PRINCESS 1:	I like the way the pattern there repeats
	The pattern here.
NATHALIE:	You ought to see my satin
	Fascinator.

PRINCESS 3:	Like the *écharpe*? Got that in
	The Champs Elysйes, *mon cher cousin.*
PRINCESS 4:	Ah yes,
	It's real *Barège.*
PRINCESS 5:	Charming.
PRINCESS 6:	Sheer loveliness.
THEIR MOTHER:	Who was that man who bowed to us?
NATHALIE:	Princess,
	That's Mr Chatsky, just arrived.
MOTHER:	Retired?
NATHALIE:	He is. Been on his travels. He desired
	To see the world, as they call it.
MOTHER:	Bachelor?
NATHALIE:	Unmarried, yes. I see I need say no more.
MOTHER:	Prince! Prince!

The **PRINCE** *inclines his ear trumpet.*

Come here! That young man there –

Nathalie Gorich knows him. Our affair

On Thursday evening – tell him he's got to come.

The **PRINCE** *hovers about* **CHATSKY,** *clearing his throat.*

I sometimes wish that God would strike them dumb,

My chattering children – crying out for a ball.

So poor Papa has to call on them all –

The eligible. Partners. *A propos* –

Is he a gentleman-in-waiting?

NATHALIE: No.

MOTHER: Well off?

NATHALIE: Far from it.

MOTHER: Prince! You come back here!

The two **COUNTESSES KHRYUMINA**, *grandmother and granddaughter, enter.*

GRANDDAUGHTER: *Grand'maman* – We're far too early. We're

                    The first arrivals.

She flounces away.

MOTHER: That's what she thinks of us.

               She's first, we don't exist. An acidulous

               Old maid she's going to be. God strike her silly.

The **GRANDDAUGHTER** *countess returns.*

GRANDDAUGHTER: M'sieu' Chatsky. Back from the sun to chilly

                    Old Moscow. Still the same?

CHATSKY: How could I change?

GRANDDAUGHTER: And you've come back unmarried?

CHATSKY: Is that strange?

               Who could I marry?

GRANDDAUGHTER: Who? You travelling men

                    Regularly pick up wives abroad, and then

                    Bring us back in-laws, more or less from hat-shops.

CHATSKY: At least they are originals, not patch-ups.

               Better to marry milliners than hats.

A number of other guests come in, among them **ZAGORETSKY**. *Clicking of heels, to-and-froing.* **SOPHIE** *appears, the guests approach her.*

GRANDDAUGHTER: *Bonsoir!* You're never punctual, and that's

So *chic*. There's something to look forward to.

ZAGORETSKY: You know about tomorrow's show. Have you

A ticket?

SOPHIE: Ticket? No.

ZAGORETSKY: Of course not.

To get one required superhuman force, not

The gentle way of commerce. All sold out.

People queue up from dawn but go without.

Asked my chum the director – but no go.

Tried everywhere and everything. You know

How I succeeded finally? Visited

An old old friend, elderly invalid,

Snatched the damned thing from him. Bad? No, that's

A blessing from him. Stay home with his cats –

Better than being miserable out.

Helpful – you know me – but I never shout

About it.

SOPHIE: Thanks for the ticket, and a double

Thank you, sir, for going to so much trouble.

More guests arrive. **ZAGORETSKY** *moves over to the gentlemen.*

ZAGORETSKY: Evening, Plato.

PLATO: Don't you Plato me.

You're a damned rogue. Go to the women. See

If you can fool them with your blasted lies.

Chatsky, old boy, I won't try to disguise

The way I feel about this swindling swine –

Anthony Zagoretsky knows how to combine

The man of the world pose with sheer villainy.

Don't play cards with the bastard sneak, for he

Will skin you solid.

ZAGORETSKY: Quite a character –

Harsh words, yes, but no real malice there.

CHATSKY: Not being honest has its compensations,

So why should you take offence? Here – execrations.

There – praise and thanks. No wonder that you grin.

PLATO: They all abuse him, but all have him in.

CHATSKY: The better to abuse him?

ZAGORETSKY *mingles with the throng.* MISS KHYLOSTOVA *comes up.*

MISS KHYLOSTOVA: Oh, hallo.

At sixty-five it's not much fun, you know,

Traipsing all the way here to see my niece.

A filthy night and not a minute's peace,

Rattling in the dark – over an hour

To get here from Pokrovka. Turns me sour –

Stomach, you know – travel. I've come up

With my little black girl and my little pup.

You see her woolly head, my dear? Perhaps

You might arrange to send them down some scraps

For supper. What a bitch she is. She spits

Like a cat. Frightens me into fits

She does, with that blackness. There, see her go

Into the maid's room. She's company, though,

She and my pupsy. Shall I call her?

SOPHIE: No.

Dear aunt, another time.

MISS KHYLOSTOVA: Like a cattle show,

They say. They have them walking up and down

In this kind of market. Where is the town?

Somewhere in Turkey. Do you know who got her

For me? That Zagoretsky.

ZAGORETSKY *comes forward but, at her next words, disappears.*

                                        Blasted rotter,

A lying gambling thief, that's all he is.

I always shoo him off my premises,

But he can get round anybody. He's

Bought these two black ones as a special favour

For me and, you know, my cousin, Parasceva,

At some fair or other, that's what they say.

But it's my belief he won them by foul play

In some filthy card game. He's all right in a way,

Though, gave me a nice present.

CHATSKY: *(loudly laughing)*   Ha. Such

Praise confers no blessing. It was too much

Even for him – he's gone.

MISS KHYLOSTOVA:	Who's the humorist?
SOPHIE:	That's Mr Chatsky.
MISS KHYLOSTOVA:	Hm. I seem to have missed

The joke. A young man laughing at the old.

Not decent. Sinful. Hm. Ought to be told.

Wait. I know him. When you were little, dear,

You danced with him. I used to pull his ear.

The little imp. I should have pulled it more.

FAMUSOV *comes in and speaks in a main voice.*

FAMUSOV: Ladies, gentlemen, we were waiting for

Prince Tugo-Ukhovsky. Here all the time

While I was waiting in the portrait gallery. I'm

Looking for Colonel Skalozub. Where's he?

Sergius Sergeyich Skalozub – easy to see.

MISS KHYLOSTOVA: He's louder than ten trumpets – deafened me.

SKALOZUB *comes in, followed, after a decent interval, by* **MOLCHALIN.**

FAMUSOV: Come on, dear Colonel Skalozub – you're late.

It's not good generalship to make us wait

So long for the battle. Here's my sister-in-law.

She knows you by repute.

MISS KHYLOSTOVA: Been here before,

Haven't you? Some regiment – the Grenadiers?

SKALOZUB: The Grand Duke's Own – the Zembla Fusiliers.

MISS KHYLOSTOVA: They're all the same to me.

SKALOZUB: Short sight perhaps?

<table>
<tr><td></td><td>Distinctive marks – piping and shoulder-straps</td></tr>
<tr><td></td><td>And gorget-patches, chevrons, badges, caps –</td></tr>
<tr><td>FAMUSOV:</td><td>Come on now, you distinguished strategist,</td></tr>
<tr><td></td><td>And dare the battle of a game of whist.</td></tr>
<tr><td></td><td>You too, dear Prince?</td></tr>
</table>

He goes, taking **SKALOZUB** *and the* **PRINCE** *with him.*

MISS KHYLOSTOVA: Never heard of the damned man.

That Colonel or General Something. How he can
Idolise that ten-foot nothingness beats me,
Your father, I mean.

MOLCHALIN: *(handing her a card)* Madame, as you see,
I've made your table up. You see, there's me
And Monsieur Kock, Tom Fomich –

MISS KHYLOSTOVA: *(getting up)* Thanks, my dear.

MOLCHALIN: What a sweet little doggy you have here.
His coat's pure silk. No bigger than a thimble,
And yet he's fierce and frolicsome and nimble.

MISS KHYLOSTOVA: Thanks for looking after him.

Many go, leaving **CHATSKY** *and* **SOPHIE** *together.*

CHATSKY: Well, well –

Oil on troubled waters.

SOPHIE: Your cracked bell
Of bitterness – can't you stop tolling it?

CHATSKY: It was meant to be sweet. Praising his exquisite
Pacification of a growling guest.

SOPHIE:	With a sting in the tail.
CHATSKY:	Come, even at their best,
	Old ladies are a fiery-tempered race.
	They need these cavaliers – a smirking face
	And squirming manners mollify their moods.
	Give them a bunch of flowers and platitudes
	And they're content. She looks as if she's sucked a
	Spoonful of sugar. Lightning conductor,
	That's what Molchalin is. All jasmine-petalled.
	See – everything is amicably settled,
	Her puppy petted, and he's nice as pie.
	While he lives, Zagoretsky will not die.
	Some time ago you eulogised about
	His virtues. Are there some that you left out?

SOPHIE *blazes as he goes away.*

SOPHIE:	Jealous, conceited, and infuriating.
	His only pleasure is humiliating.
	He makes me mad.
MR N:	*(coming up to her):* You've something on your mind?
SOPHIE:	Yes, Mr Chatsky.
MR N:	Chatsky, do you find
	He's changed since he came back?
SOPHIE:	Yes, for the worse.
	His mind seems to have suffered a reverse.
MR N:	He's off his head, you mean?

SOPHIE: *(after a pause)* Did I say that?

MR N: But there are symptoms?

SOPHIE: *(with a hard look)* So it seems.

MR N: But at

His age? Really –

SOPHIE: (Now. Try that for size,

Dear Mr Chatsky. She how the libel flies

Already. You love dressing people down

Or up, in the costume of a stupid clown.

So see now how the costume fits on you.)

She goes off.

MR N: He's off his head. She seems to think it's true.

Where did she get it? Must be something in it.

Enter MR D.

You heard?

MR D: Heard what?

MR N: Just got the news this minute.

Poor Chatsky's off his head.

MR D: That's tommy rot.

MR N: It's not just me that's saying it.

MR D: They're not

Shouting it from the rooftops, are they, though?

Leave that to you.

MR N: Somebody's sure to know.

I'll get confirmation.

He goes off.

MR D: That damned scandalmonger.

I never saw such a perverted hunger

For garbage.

ZAGORETSKY *comes in.*

Heard about Chatsky?

ZAGORETSKY: Tell me.

MR D: He's

Off his head.

ZAGORETSKY: Ah yes. It's one of these

Sad cases that you sometimes hear about.

Locked in the madhouse, but they let him out.

His wicked uncle had him certified,

Chained up and left alone to rot inside.

Of course, he may have escaped. One wonders how.

MR D: Good heavens, he was in this room just now.

Dear Zagoretsky, we don't need newspapers

When we have you. Said something about escape? As

Easy as that? Is it possible?

ZAGORETSKY: Easy enough.

He bit through the chain. These madmen can be tough.

MR D: I must look into this. But – mum's the word.

Off he goes.

ZAGORETSKY: Which of them here is Chatsky? Seem to have heard

The name somewhere.

The **GRANDDAUGHTER** *countess enters.*

                                   You hear about him?

GRANDDAUGHTER: Who?

ZAGORETSKY: Chatsky.

GRANDDAUGHTER: Oh, we had a word or two.

ZAGORETSKY: Felicitations on your escape from danger.

He's off his head.

GRANDDAUGHTER: Ah. I saw something strange, a

Kind of glint of lunacy in his eyes.

So. I was right.

Her **GRANDMOTHER** *comes in.*

                    Grand'maman, such a surprise,

Such gorgeous news.

GRANDMOTHER: *Ja? Lauter, mein* dear.

You know *ich habe* this blockage in *mein* ear.

Ich kann nicht hear.

GRANDDAUGHTER: I must get confirmation.

He'll make you *au fait* with the situation.

She runs off.

GRANDMOTHER: Whatever is it? Is the house on fire?

ZAGORETSKY: No. But the incendiary risk couldn't be higher.

Chatsky's the trouble.

GRANDMOTHER: Chatsky's in trouble, you said?

Is he in jail?

ZAGORETSKY: A bullet hit his head

On operations, lodged, and turned his reason.

GRANDMOTHER: In the Freemasons' Lodge he turned a heathen?

That what you said?

ZAGORETSKY: Never mind, never mind.

He goes off.

GRANDMOTHER: Mr Zagoretsky! Clever mind – that kind

Of mind goes quickest.

Enter the PRINCE.

Treat him very shoddy,

They do, poor Prince. Hardly a breath in his body

But they drag him round to balls. Prince! Did you hear?

PRINCE: Ah? Hm?

GRANDMOTHER: He's deaf, poor soul. Tell me, my dear,

Are the police here yet?

PRINCE: Eh? Hm?

GRANDMOTHER: Are they here,

The police? Who took Mr Chatsky away

And put him in jail?

PRINCE: Oh? Hm?

GRANDMOTHER: It's private's pay

For him. Reduced to the ranks. Sidearms and rifle.

Round the square at the double. Shouldn't trifle

With things like religion. Lost his faith. Voltaire

Has always been the trouble. Once you breathe an

Ounce of his foul air in – bang! – you're a heathen.

87

A heathen! Do you hear?

PRINCE: Oo? Hm?

GRANDMOTHER: There, there,

You're deaf, little father. Leave it or lump it,

I've said what I've said. Get your blasted trumpet.

Deafness is a sin.

The company enters, chattering.

MISS KHYLOSTOVA: Mad, then – just like that –

Descended on his head – a sort of hat

You could call it. You heard, Sophie dear?

PLATO: Who started this?

NATHALIE: Oh, everyone, darling.

PLATO: We're

Forced to believe it then. But I have my doubts.

FAMUSOV *comes in.*

FAMUSOV: Doubts? About mad Chatsky? The man who shouts

And clouts and flouts Authority? It was I

That found him out. I was the first. Just try

Telling him about our duty to defer

To the higher powers. My God, you stir

A nest of scorpions up. And those that are

Properly deferential to the Czar –

He calls them sycophants, lickspittles, toadies.

MISS KHYLOSTOVA: Yes. That is madness. Yes. Just now it showed. His

Manner of guffawing at some slight remark.

MOLCHALIN: He asked me to defect from Moscow Arch—

Ives.

GRANDDAUGHTER: He compared me to a milliner.

NATHALIE: Said we should vegetate like what we were —

Vegetables.

ZAGORETSKY: Mad all right.

GRANDDAUGHTER: It's in his eyes.

FAMUSOV: Look at his lineage. It's no surprise.

His mother had eight terrible attacks

Of madness.

MISS KHYLOSTOVA: It's the drink. Alcohol cracks

The vital membranes.

PRINCESS: Drink, yes.

GRANDDAUGHTER: Yes, it's drink.

MISS KHYLOSTOVA: Drink. Now I come to think, he wouldn't blink

At swigging champagne from the bottle.

GRANDDAUGHTER: By the

Magnum.

ZAGORETSKY: Pardon me, ladies, surely neither

Of you is right. The hundred-gallon cask.

FAMUSOV: Let's have our drink. It's not too much to ask.

There's not much harm in having a drop too much.

It's reading, learning, studying and such

That harm the human brain, crack it to fractions,

Producing crazy thoughts and crazy actions.

MISS KHYLOSTOVA: You're right. It's education. Pure pollution.

Making them overthrow the Constitution.

PRINCESS: A constitute – no, it's an institute

In Petersburg. Know what they do? Recruit

Atheists as professors. A poor relation

Of mine received a godless education

In chemistry and botany at that place.

He'll puff the stuff like smoke into your face.

Anatomy – he'll talk of your inside.

Hates women, even me, and can't abide

The services that keep our country great.

SKALOZUB: I think I've got good news for you. The State,

So they say, proposes to militarise

Our schools and kill the atheistic lies

Lurking in books. In army-style they'll do

Everything by numbers – one two, one two!

There'll be a book or so there, I suppose,

The Bible, say, censored of course, for those

Who've had the devil properly drilled out.

FAMUSOV: Ah no, dear Colonel, cousin. Can you doubt

The only way is – cut the Gordian knot.

Impound all books, then burn the blasted lot.

ZAGORETSKY: There's books and books – of course, you will agree.

Now, if they gave the Censor's job to me –

Take children's books – animals on a farm

And suchlike. Some say there's no real harm

In tales of animals, all tusks and teeth –

Bears, lions, elephants. Look underneath,

It's social mockery. Know what they are,

These books? Injunctions to put down the Czar.

MISS KHYLOSTOVA: But, gentlemen, whether it's books or booze,

Chatsky's stark staring mad. We ought to use

A little Christian charity – compassion.

He was a clever man, after his fashion.

He has a name they used to venerate.

He has three hundred souls on his estate.

FAMUSOV: Four hundred.

MISS KHYLOSTOVA: Three.

FAMUSOV: Four hundred.

MISS KHYLOSTOVA: Three.

FAMUSOV: I've got

The agricultural survey.

MISS KHYLOSTOVA: Tommy rot.

FAMUSOV: Four, four, you ignorant woman.

MISS KHYLOSTOVA: Don't ignorant me,

You ignorant man. I know these things, you see.

FAMUSOV: Look here, it's four.

MISS KHYLOSTOVA: It's three, it's three, it's three.

NATHALIE: See. He's coming in.

He is indeed.

ALL: Shhhh.

MISS KHYLOSTOVA: And if a fit comes on,

What'll we do?

They all back away.

FAMUSOV: You take your three and be gone.

Look here, dear chap, you're not at all the thing.

Not enough sleep, and too much travelling.

You're ill. Let's feel your pulse.

CHATSKY: I've been felt enough –

My chest is sore from bear hugs, hairy and rough.

My waist from bowing and my ears with screams.

As for my head – its poor grey cortex seems

Bursting with the fatuous – or mad.

They look at each other on that last word. **CHATSKY** *addresses* **SOPHIE.**

Lost in the crowd. And desperately sad.

Yes, Moscow saddens me.

MISS KHYLOSTOVA: Moscow's to blame,

FAMUSOV: Naturally.

Keep away from him, Sophie.

CHATSKY: Just the same,

Moscow. If not worse.

SOPHIE: What's making you cross?

CHATSKY: Oh nothing really. Really it's a loss

Of faith.

More knowing looks.

A little Frenchman from Bordeaux,

Puffed up, rotund, one of the tribe who know

Their own superiority, had quite an assembly

Around him, while he told how he was trembly

With apprehension, off to barbarous Russia.

But all he found was kindness, such a crush, a

Crowd, a cram of hospitality.

I'm still in *la belle France, oui, mes amis.*

Nothing but French – the food, the conversation,

The ladies' dresses. All this imitation

Makes him a kind of king of the imitated.

"France, ah, lovely France!" They were elated,

These young princesses, reared on Francomania.

Russia, Siberia, Latvia, Lithuania –

All rubbish. Me, I stood some way away

And, meekly, audibly, began to pray

That the good Russian God might strike and slay

This damned servility, these xenophiles,

Who lard their lardy jowls with smirks and smiles

Whenever anywhere but here is mentioned.

Abroad. Ah, Europe. Europe is the French and

Any nation properly Gallicised.

They call me "bigot", one of the despised

Race of the obscurantists when I say

That Russia should pursue the Russian way.

We drop our customs, ancient holiness,

Our noble language and our Northern dress,

Scraping our chins, powdered like babies' bums,

Aping each little crowing cock who comes

From France. "Can you translate *Mademoiselle*?

Madame? Such terms cannot be rendered well

Into the barbarous Russian tongue." Oh God,

I say, try *sudarynya*. They: How odd,

Oh, what a joke. It's not enough to scoff –

They laugh their wretched Frenchified heads off.

I think of a reply. They go away.

Anyone who has anything to say

Home-brewed, true Russian, from the Russian soul,

The Russian soil, can go and dig a hole,

Shove himself in it. Let him be so bold

As wish to tell the world – lo and behold.

Lo and behold –

He sees that the old are playing cards and the young vigorously dancing something French.

CURTAIN

Act Four

The entrance hall of **FAMUSOV**'s *mansion. The main staircase descends into it. Below, on the right, the Porter's lodge and doors leading to the porch. On the left,* **MOLCHALIN**'s *room. Night. Some footmen bustle, others doze, awaiting their masters. A footman precedes the two countesses, grandmother and granddaughter, as they descend.*

FOOTMAN: The Countess Khryumin's carriage.

GRANDDAUGHTER: Famusov's ball.

Not much dancing. No one to dance with. All

Weird, most of them old as the Twelve Apostles.

A palaeontological museum – full of fossils.

GRANDMOTHER: Oh, let's get home. Let me get into my grave.

I said last time, after that ball he gave,

I'd roll up like a ball and roll away.

They leave and drive off. **PLATO** *and* **NATHALIE GORICH** *appear with a fussy footman.*

FIRST FOOTMAN: Carriage for Major Gorich.

NATHALIE: Not too gay,

My Plato-poppet, are you? It was fun.

Wasn't it?

PLATO: Balls? I'd hit them, every one,

Over the moon if I were strong enough.

They're soporific, they're a lot of stuff

And nonsense. I don't object, my little beauty.

But still – past midnight, and I'm still on duty.

Ordered to dance, I dance. It's not much pleasure.

Except for you, I suppose.

NATHALIE: My tiresome treasure,

Are you trying to be old before your time?

PLATO: I'm getting bored with this same old pantomime.

Acting the happy husband. Some are born to it.

Me, no.

NATHALIE *has left with the footman, who now returns to* PLATO.

FOOTMAN: Sir. Madame is waiting. She's a bit –

You know, begging your pardon, sir.

PLATO: *(sighing)*   I'm there.

They go off. CHATSKY *appears with his footman, who goes off at his master's command.*

CHATSKY: Tell them to bring it and be quick. The air

Is full of misty spectres, dying hopes.

And I? A fighter staggering on the ropes.

Inept. A weakling. What did I think I'd find?

A happy cry? Mind calling to mind?

Arms about me? Love? A metaphor:

I'm in my carriage, shut between door and door,

Roof and floor, mile after mile after mile

Of plain, empty, barren. To beguile

The empty brain, an insubstantial thing –

Blue or blueish, shapeless, shimmering –

Somehow arises on the road ahead.

I follow it – one hour, two hours, all the dead

Day of travel – but there's nothing there.

Freezing air, the steppe, brainless, bare –

Mirage, frustration...

His footman returns.

Is it ready yet?

FOOTMAN: Can't find the coachman, sir.

CHATSKY: He's drunk, I bet.

Get out and look for him. We can't stay here

All night.

The footman goes. **REPETILOV** *comes running from the porch. He falls, picks himself up, muttering.*

REPETILOV: Stupid, putting that step there. My dear

Friend, stranger. Let me rub my eyes. *Mon cher,*

Where did your spectre rise from? You know, they go

On about me, when I say I know

The future – omens and presentiments,

That sort of thing – premonitory dents

In that great blank wall. But somehow I knew

That if I hurried here there would be *you.*

So, let them laugh at that, and you laugh too.

The superstitious fool who claims to peel off

The skin of what's to come. Old Repetilov.

What drew me to you? Perhaps something magnetic,

A kind of love, empathy, empathetic

Attraction. I'm your friend. I am your dear

Dear friend, transported, sort of, here.

I won't abandon you, though all abandon

Poor Repetilov. I give you my hand on

That. I swear it. May God strike me dead

If it's not true.

CHATSKY: You struck yourself instead.

REPETILOV: Laugh at me if you like. You don't like me,

Even if I love *you*. You know, I can be

Indifferent to the others. But when I

See you, I go all risible, tongue-tied, shy.

Why, I wonder.

CHATSKY: Self-depreciation

In your case merits different motivation.

REPETILOV: I know. Scold me, curse me. Like the patriarch Job

I curse the day I was set on this spinning globe.

The time I've squandered – I say what *is* the time?

CHATSKY: Time for your bed. The ball is over. I'm

Afraid if you endeavour to assay

The climb, you'll have to come down right away.

REPETILOV: Balls, eh? What good are they? They're just a joke.

We'll never crack the shoulder-cracking yoke

Of social convention unless unless – we what?

Did you read that book about it?

CHATSKY: Surely you're not

Reading books? Books are a world you seal off

From what you call the real, dear Repetilov.

REPETILOV: Call me a Vandal, call me a Visigoth,

A philistine, a palpitating moth

That flits around life's lamp. It's all too true.

Dinner parties, dances, gambling – you

Name it – Been unfaithful to my wife,

Battered my offspring, mortgaged my very life,

Had all my property put in sequestration,

Thrown in the lock-up – belligerent intoxication

They called it. Kept a dancing girl – three, in fact –

Four to a bed. Renounced the law, attacked

Religion. Always drunk. Nine nights on end

Drunk. A devastating record.

CHATSKY: Come, my friend,

Don't make me feel more desperate than I do.

REPETILOV: But I've repented, changed, reformed. So you

Ought to congratulate me, not condemn.

I've met some sober people. It's with them

I spend my evenings now. Intelligent,

That's what they are. It's heaven. It's heaven-sent,

A revelation.

CHATSKY: To judge from tonight's amount

Of liquor –

REPETILOV: Oh, the odd night doesn't count.

Now, ask me where I've been.

CHATSKY: That I can guess.

The Club?

REPETILOV:	The English Club. Let me confess,
	Although I'm pledged to the strictest secrecy,
	I've joined what's called a clandestine society.
	Now keep that to yourself. Each Thursday we
	Have this special session.
CHATSKY:	You frighten me.
	If you spread this information about,
	You and your secrets are going to be chucked out.
REPETILOV:	Don't worry. Even when we shout aloud,
	Nobody understands. It's a wonderful crowd.
	We discuss everything – juries and parliaments,
	Lord Byron. Even I feel pretty dense
	Sometimes, hold my tongue, sit still and listen.
	But something's missing, and it's you we miss, an
	Exceptional intelligence. Come along, then.
	I'll introduce you to these kings of men,
	Crème de la crème, and not like me a bit.
	The talk is on. Dive in the midst of it.
CHATSKY:	The hell with that. At this hour? Have some sense.
	I need some sleep.
REPETILOV:	That's one of our arguments –
	Sleep as a waste of time. Whoever goes
	To bed these days? Time enough for repose
	When we have lived. We're living. We're the kind
	Of men who live the life of the living mind.

We're fire – the Fiery Dozen is what we're called.

Talk about balls – we bawl. Sometimes we've bawled

Loud as a regiment.

CHATSKY: What's the frenzy for?

REPETILOV: We're animated, animated. More

Than animated.

CHATSKY: All you do is be animated?

REPETILOV: I can't explain it now. What we've debated

And still debate is the function of the State.

Something is going to happen, friend. Just wait.

You must meet Prince Gregory. Yes, he's an odd one.

Unique. There's no one like the man. By God, one

Of these days he'll make us die of laughing.

Talks like an Englishman, telegraphing

As they do – click click click click through his teeth.

His hair's cropped like a convict's – underneath

There's real conviction. Do you know Vorkulov?

By God, there's a voice. A walking singing school of

Bel canto. *"Ah, non lasciarmi, no, no, no."*

Remarkable. Then there's Boris and Leo,

Twins, you know, but they don't share a brain,

Have enough for quadruplets. Then again

There's Hippolytus Marcellovich Udъshev.

A breathing living genius. The true chef

Of the intellectual kitchen. You know his works?

He doesn't write now. Chap like that that shirks

His intellectual duty should be lashed,

Bashed, smashed, bloody well gored and gashed,

And told with every stroke to write, write, write.

I read a thing of his the other night

– A piece called "Something". What's the thing about?

Everything, that's what. For there's no doubt

The swine knows everything. I don't suppose

You'd know Count Theodore Tolstoy? One of those

Who always say they're going to write some day,

And if not leave it to a descendant. May

The good God strike me dead this instant if

He's not the greatest living Russian. Stiff

As a ramrod, a great fighter of duels,

Set on by the most inflammable of fuels

To rob and rape. He was exiled to Kamchatka,

But it wasn't long before he got out of that, ca–

Reening round, transformed to an Aleutian.

Criminality is his solution

To Russia's problems. But hear him orate

On Honour. It's incredible the state

He whips himself to. Eyes and face on fire.

He weeps, we sob. Would you seriously require

A better image of the high demonic?

Such men. By God, they're like an iron tonic.

Of course, I'm nothing in comparison.

But if I turn the mental engine on,

It sometimes pops up with a little pun.

You'd think I'd fired a great creative gun

The way the others seize on it. There's six

To decorate it with dramatic tricks

And six to write the music for it. When

The thing's performed – well, all these marvellous men

Cheer till their throats go raw and clap their paws.

I'm proud. You never heard such damned applause.

God didn't give me much ability,

God knows. A good heart, though. They seem to be

Fond of me and never go pooh-pooh

When I blurt out the stupid things I do.

FOOTMAN: *(by the porch)*

Carriage for Colonel Skalozub.

REPETILOV: For who?

SKALOZUB *comes down.* **REPETILOV** *runs towards him.* **CHATSKY** *sneaks off.*

Why, Colonel, this is more than we deserve. Es–

teemed sir, they said it was active service

You were on. But here you are. All ready for

A marvellous time. At the Club. Need I say more

Than this: Prince Gregory is the centre

Of a fine intellectual crowd. We enter,

They fill us with champagne, and then they start.

It's going to warm the cockles of your heart.

Not cockles, no – poor people's food. You'll hear

Ideas that you and I have no idea

About.

SKALOZUB: Clear off. Don't want your damned ideas.

You're thick. And what you want is two thick ears.

But if you like I'll send my sergeant-major.

He'll do a real Voltaire on you, I wager,

You and that blasted atheist Prince Gregory.

Like new recruits we've rescued out of beggary

He'll fall you in and march you bloody towsers

Until your ideas drop into your trousers.

REPETILOV: You've nothing but the Service on your mind,

Have you? You've done all right. Some of us find

It's not so easy to climb up the ladder.

Take my sad case. You'll never find a sadder.

I was under that blasted Baron von Klotz.

He was hatching up his gloomy German plots

To climb up to a ministerial post.

I tried to be his son-in-law. Like most

Young civil servants I soon fouled my anchor.

Von Klotz had this big house on the Fontanka.

I moved in next to him – that cost a packet.

Soon I was fiddling with his daughter's placket.

We had to marry. Did I get a job?

Oh no. Just a scrap of dowry. That slob

Was scared of favouring his own relations.

For Germany excels all other nations

In having clean ideals and filthy policies.

His daughter – she was not the best of solaces

For me, that had to see each snotnosed pusher

Of pen and self take over blasted Russia –

The bureaucratic Czars. I've had a look

In the Petersburg Directory – damned big book –

There they all are. Vanity, all is vanity.

Promotion, decorations, sheer insanity,

Inanity. Humanity's visceral faults

Need bloody purging with a dose of salts.

He sees that **SKALOZUB** *has been replaced by* **ZAGORETSKY.**

ZAGORETSKY: Do please go on. I'm of the liberal tribe,

So must applaud your eloquent dia – ha ha – tribe.

I've suffered too. I never took a bribe,

Opposed corruption with a well-aimed gibe.

Look at me now.

REPETILOV: You ought to be Skalozub.

Or was it Chatsky? Give the lamp a rub –

They disappear like genies.

ZAGORETSKY: What do you think

Of Chatsky?

REPETILOV: We've a kind of common link –

Serious people, both of us. He's bright.

I had a chat with him – was it tonight? –

Yes, we talked about the music hall –

A wonderful institution. What they call

Real culture. All the rest can go to hell.

ZAGORETSKY: Didn't he strike you as being rather – well,

Deranged?

REPETILOV: Nonsense.

ZAGORETSKY: But that's what they all say.

REPETILOV: Balderdash.

ZAGORETSKY: Ask anybody.

REPETILOV: It's they

That want their heads examined.

ZAGORETSKY: If you're unconvinced,

Here come the heads of society – see, Prince T–

ugo-Ukhovsky and the Princesses.

REPETILOV: All rot.

Those noble personages have appeared. Footman abound.

ZAGORETSKY: Your ladyships, is it true or is it not

That Chatsky's mad?

PRINCESS 1: Mad as a hare or hatter.

PRINCESS 2: No doubt about it.

PRINCESS 3: Everyone knows that, a

Matter of common knowledge. The Khvorovs, as well as

The Dryanskoys, Varlyanskys, Skachkovs –

PRINCESS 4: Tell us

Something new.

PRINCESS 5: Stale as this morning's bread.

ZAGORETSKY: Confirmed, then. Mr Chatsky's off his head.

But here's a man who won't believe it.

PRINCESS 6: You!

You go against the rest of us? It's true.

Has to be true if everyone says so.

REPETILOV: I beg your pardons, ladies. I didn't know

That it was common knowledge.

MISS KHLYOSTOVA *comes down on the arm of* **MOLCHALIN.**

OLD PRINCESS: Common, you say?

The common madhouse, that's for him. Why, they

Should have shut that lunatic away

Ages ago. His talk – it makes one wince.

Thinks he knows more than all of us, even the Prince

Here. It's pure Voltaire. Chatsky! Let's see.

Prince, you take Zizi. The rest come with me

In the six-seater. Off we go.

MISS KHYLOSTOVA: Princess!

Our little settlement.

OLD PRINCESS: Settlement, yes.

If you're referring to the small amount

I lost at cards, put it to my account.

ALL: Goodbye. Goodbye. Goodbye. Goodbye. Goodbye.

The Prince's family leaves. So does **ZAGORETSKY**.

REPETILOV: It's terrible. Poor devil. The mind climbs high,

Gives out for lack of oxygen. Why try?

Life's a long trial, very trying.

MISS KHYLOSTOVA: I'm sure

It's a judgment. Maybe there's a cure.

But as for you, my dear, I think that you're

Past hope. Molchalin – there's your cubby-hole.

I don't need seeing off. God bless.

MOLCHALIN *goes into his room.*

                               You'll roll

From gutter to grave one of these days, Repetilov.

So settle down, my dear, and try to peel off

The skin of debauchery. Then you'd be showing

The fruity you that's hidden. Yes? I'm going.

She goes.

REPETILOV: Where can I go? The morning's inching up.

Another bottle? Well, say half a cup.

A dram. A drop. To keep out the cold air.

Hey, you. Come on, you. Drive me off somewhere.

He leaves with his **FOOTMAN***. The last lamp goes out.* **CHATSKY** *comes from the porter's lodge.*

CHATSKY: Can I believe my ears? It wasn't fun.

It was pure malice. How then was it done?

What mad conductor gave the initial beat

To start this fugue off? Chorus, let's repeat

That phrase. He's mad, he's mad. They're gratified

To think it. Could one but pierce the bestial hide

And see the real animal inside,

What would be worse? The heart? The rotten roots

Of the tongue? How come these putrid fruits

That hang upon the tree of divine speech?

It isn't one that wants it. They all reach,

Each and every one of them, to pluck

The rotten apple. And the juice they suck

Becomes the juice they spit. Sound the alarm!

Truth is abroad, and it can do us harm!

Public opinion. My native land.

God help us. Less than a day. No, an hour, and

Already it's enough, more than enough.

Sophie – she too can't have been clawed by that rough

Beast of calumny. They told her, no doubt.

She breathed in the bad air, then breathed it out.

Amused her, perhaps. Though not particularly

Because the calumny attached to me.

She feels the same for everyone, I know.

Meaning that she feels nothing. Let it go.

That fainting fit she had? It seemed a sign

Of pain for someone else's pain. Not mine.

The vapours. Girlish nerves. The least thing harms them.

A trifle sets them off – a trifle calms them.

Deep feeling? No. She'd wilt, quiver, quail

– Collapse if someone trod on a cat's tail.

SOPHIE *appears above, with a candle.*

SOPHIE: Mr Molchalin, are you there?

She closes the door hurriedly.

CHATSKY: Oh, no!

Not her! My head – I saw her come, then go.

My blood seethes. Fantasy? Am I really mad?

No vision, no. Molchalin. So they had

A tryst arranged...

His **FOOTMAN** *appears.*

FOOTMAN: The carriage.

CHATSKY *pushes him back outside.*

CHATSKY: Nor good or bad,

I'll wait. Till even the sun comes up.

Hand me the poison. And I'll drain the cup.

Better to see all, know all. Here and now.

He hides behind a pillar. **LIZA** *appears from above with a candle.*

LIZA: Brrrr. I'm a bit scared. This place somehow

Fills up with boggarts when the lights are out.

Funny she thought she saw him mooning about

Down here. That Mr Chatsky, that is. Like a spy,

Or speck of dirt in the corner of her eye,

She fancies that he follows her. He's gone.

Shut up his love and put his nightshirt on.

And now it's her love that's on the – what? – agenda.

Knock knock. See what the good Lord's going to send her.

She knocks on **MOLCHALIN**'s *door.*

You there? She's calling. Come on, open the door, you.

Quick, before someone sees. She's waiting for you.

MOLCHALIN *comes out, yawning, stretching.* **SOPHIE** *appears above and starts to creep downstairs.* **CHATSKY** *remains immobile and unseen.*

LIZA:　　　　Bit stony-hearted, aren't you – icy?

MOLCHALIN:　　　　　　　　　　　　Towards you?

Never, never, Liza.

LIZA:　　　　　　　　　　Referring to

Her.

MOLCHALIN:　　　　　Forget her for the moment. Why

Doesn't something sometime get into your eye –

You know – a flash of passion. Why no rush

Of feeling in your face – no blush, no flush?

You want to be a servant all your life,

Hiding your true emotions?

LIZA:　　　　　　　　　　　　Seek a wife,

They say, and first be disciplined.

You look like something swaying in the wind.

Tousled, yawning, blinking in this light.

You can be sleepy on your wedding night.

MOLCHALIN:　　Wedding? Who with?

LIZA:	With her.
MOLCHALIN:	Ah, get away.

It's just to pass the time. A wedding day?
You must be joking. I've got my career
To think about.

LIZA: I can't be – What's this I hear?
She's set on getting wed.

MOLCHALIN: That's as may be,
But I'm damned if she is going to be wed to me.
There's a big thing that really turns me off
And makes me shudder. If old Famusov
Saw us at it – God, what a to-do.
Liza, you know I tell it straight to you.
Little Sophie – well, she's not my type.
All right for them that like their fruit unripe.
Good luck to her, but not with me. She'd drop
Yours truly like she put that big full stop
To what she felt for Chatsky. She's like that.
My heart goes cold when I see her. Pit-a-pat
When I see you.

LIZA: You ought to be ashamed.

MOLCHALIN: I don't see that. You mean I've got to be blamed
For following my old dad's good advice?
Gave it me on his deathbed. Son, be nice
To everybody, that's what he said. Your boss,

	Your colleagues, landlord. And it's no dead loss
	To be agreeable to the whole damned catalogue
	– Laundresses, boot-black, even the porter's dog.
LIZA:	You've got a lot of people to take care of.
MOLCHALIN:	And this, you see, explains the whole affair of
	Me and her. Acting the part to please
	The daughter of the man who –

LIZA: Oversees

Your pay, promotion, bed and blooming board
And drink as well.

MOLCHALIN: So where's the harm? Good Lord,

Girl, where's the harm? Come here a minute.

Give me a hug and shove your whole heart in it.

She pushes him away.

Why couldn't she be you?

He is about to go, but **SOPHIE** *prevents him.*

SOPHIE: Don't move from there.

I've heard more than enough. Horror. The sheer

Horror of it.

MOLCHALIN: Miss Sophie!

SOPHIE: Don't you speak

One word. I could do anything. I could wreak

Havoc.

MOLCHALIN *is on his knees.* **SOPHIE** *pushes him away.*

MOLCHALIN: Don't be angry. Look at me.

I swear −

SOPHIE: You'd swear more lies. I want to be

Left alone. More lies. Music to clothe them.

I want no memories. I hate them. Loathe them.

MOLCHALIN: *(grovelling at her feet)*

Forgive −

SOPHIE: Don't be the worm you are.

MOLCHALIN: One word −

SOPHIE: I know your words. All lies, lies, I've heard

Enough of you.

MOLCHALIN: It was my little joke.

SOPHIE: Keep away. You're going to be sorry you spoke.

Stand off. Or else I'll scream and wake the house.

MOLCHALIN: No −

He stifles himself, rising.

SOPHIE: I've heard of lice but never seen a louse.

But now I see one. Don't expect me to cry,

Reproach, complain. You're just not worth it.

Say this only: Leave this house and then

Vanish. I don't want to hear of you again.

MOLCHALIN: I obey. Your. Order.

SOPHIE: Or would you rather

I told the whole filthy story to my father?

It doesn't much matter what becomes of me.

Go. No, don't. Stay in your post and be

A model of obsequiousness, and know

Somebody's sick to see you. You were so

Audacious, weren't you? Meaning crooked-minded.

Your littleness. I'm glad that I could find it

Out in black night, not in the press of day

Among the disapproving. As when they

Saw me faint. Mr Chatsky more than any –

CHATSKY: *(flinging himself between them)*

Go on and faint, you sham. There won't be many

Better occasions –

LIZA *has dropped her candle in fright.* **MOLCHALIN** *dashes off to his room.*

So – you spat out me

To make a meal of that. I tried to see

Reason in it, virtue. A plausible cause

For holding back rage. Sheathing claws.

Scuttles away, does he, crablike. For him

Modesty capsized, old trust grew dim.

Who can guess what Fate is up to? She

– Vicious, vindictiveness to sensibility –

Blesses the Molchalins of this world.

SOPHIE: Don't go on. I'm ready to have hurled

All possible reproach. I'll do the throwing.

The deceit, the deceit –

She is now Niobe.

LIZA: Oh God, Oh God, there's going

To be an almighty rumpus. He loves a row.

Your father –

FAMUSOV *comes in with a crowd of candle-bearing servants.*

FAMUSOV: Candles, lanterns! Come on now,

Hurry hurry hurry. Burglars, eh?

The faces – familiar. What have you got to say,

Sophie, you brazen bitch? Just like your mother –

Quick to deceive, one as bad as the other.

Get the old man out of the way – intrigue,

Intrigue. But you're in a more ingenious league.

Said he was mad. That was a brilliant plot,

Clever of the two of you, was it not?

Made a fool of me, fools of my friends,

Distinguished guests.

CHATSKY: God, it never ends –

My sick amazement. So – you did that too?

That too was your invention?

FAMUSOV: As for you,

I shan't be taken in again. Go on then, fight.

Let the damned charade of the damned night

Greet the damned dawn. You – you blatherskite –

He deals a slap to a servant. To the porter he speaks.

This is the moron that I made a porter.

Deaf and dumb and blind. Just when he ought to

Keep his ears clean and his peepers skinned,

Like bits of garbage blowing on the wind,

In come the dregs. I suppose you sauntered off

To down a dram or have a spit and cough

And an illegal drag. I'll have you sent,

Both of you, to the Penal Settlement.

You'd sell your master, would you – blood and bones?

Now you can break your bodies breaking stones.

To LIZA:

And, you shifty-eyed bitch, had a great time,

Haven't you? Moscow's taught you. Cream of the crime

Creeps here, dressed in its best. You were quick to learn.

Playing the bawd, procuring. What did you earn

From that, eh? Take my word, you're going to burn.

But first you're going to freeze. Back to your hovel,

Feed the chickens. Groan and gripe and grovel.

Clear out.

To SOPHIE:

And you, you pool of slimy water

Dignified by being my darling daughter,

Just wait a day or two. You're not exempted

From doing penance. Tempted, weren't you, tempted

By rakes and rogues and rips? There's no temptation

Where you'll be going to. Look for salvation

In Saratov province, staying with your aunt.

Read the lives of the saints. Knit. Sew. You shan't

Find in the windy wilds fresh ways to blight

Your blooming innocence. Serenades in the night?

You'll get those from the wolves.

To **CHATSKY**:

                                          And now you, sir.

Wish I could do to you what I'll do to her.

You've spoken plain to me, so I'll be plain.

Don't dare to darken these damned doors again.

Neither the back door, nor the front or side.

I tell you, sir, I shan't be satisfied

Till every Moscow door's shut in your face.

I'll publicise your blasted blatant base

Buggerings about all over Russia.

By God I will. I'll raise the alarm. I'll push a

Writ through the Supreme Court. I'll see you are

Thrown to the lions. And that means the Czar.

A silence, except for tears and panting.

CHATSKY: I don't quite understand. I'm being chidden,

But there's another message – sort of hidden,

And still not clear when it comes out of hiding.

I'm on an insubstantial horse and riding

In the wrong direction. It's been a long long day.

I came in innocence? Ignorance. Poured away

My heart's blood down the drain. In a passionate tumble

The words went clattering – holy, heartfelt, humble

On you – you – you! You led me on,

Unscrupulous. If you'd said the chance was gone

That would have been – well, that. You could have said

Our past together was a joke. The dead

Memories a stale jar of pot-pourri.

But the past doesn't die. Alive in me,

I thought it was alive in you. You could

Have said, and I would have understood,

My reappearance was not just surprising

But sickening. (Yet you were disguising

Revulsion at my acts, my thoughts, my words.)

Then, though belated, I would have joined the birds

That migrate from our winter. Smelt the cold

And flown. Well, well. Creep in your cell. You've sold

Potential sweetness to a slavering clown.

You'll think a little. Cool your anger down,

Forgive him, seek a double resuscitation.

For why should you destroy yourself? Your station

In life is long decreed – the Moscow lady,

Whose vital patterns come to her ready-made. He

Will be the lapdog, errand boy, whipping boy,

Fusion of slobbering slave and tatty toy.

The ideal Moscow husband. My lady's page

And all you'll need to read. I've cooled my rage,

Reverted to indifference. Spoken. Broken

With my past dreams. A future has awoken.

For you too, little father, one in which

A more acceptable dog will sniff the bitch

On offer. An obsequious operator,

Oily and smooth, prototypical head waiter

Worthy of the man he waits on. He

Will devastate his father-in-law-to-be.

You worship rank. Well, he'll be rank all right.

Doze on, doze on. The real world's bugs won't bite.

Your pillow is the ignorance of bliss,

Bliss of ignorance. Enough of this.

Dream on. I've had my dreams. My eyes are wide

Open. They look amazed at the world outside –

The world of father, daughter, brainless lover,

The whole damned boiling – I mean *damned*. Take cover.

I'll fire the cannon of my long frustration.

Or will I? Yielding to fate's dispensation,

I accepted a hell of cursers, persecutors,

Treachery, lechery, sneerers, liars, looters,

Rooters out of scandal, the beam in the eye

Unseen by the mote-hunters. All the sly

And sinister, the scandal-dandlers, drooling

Old fops that have our destinies for ruling,

Old raddled dames that plot and plot. Your world,

Curled up in your own rottenness. You hurled

The libel of my madness like a brick

To smash my window. If to be sane is sick,

I revel in my sound insanity. Breathe

Your air? Eat your victuals? Nod at your nonsense? Wreathe

The weedy garlands of your triumphs round

My head? And think to hear a rational sound

From your cracked vessel? Good. You're sane. I'm mad.

Moscow is bad. The whole world may be bad,

But somewhere there must be a nook, a niche,

Where sanity is let off from the leash,

The brain can breathe. I'll ride this way no more.

Fare well. Fare ill. Why should I care? Send for

My carriage. Carriage.

He leaves. Soon he is heard being driven away.

FAMUSOV: Well – didn't I say he was off his head?

God – you should have heard the things he said.

Oily, smooth – father-in-law – what he meant

I can't work out. Moscow – truculent,

So damned truculent. The world's in a shocking way.

And so am I. What are they going to say?

Prince, the Princess, the princesses and

The colonel – general. Nobody will understand

My poor predicament. Oh my God. In a bad way.

Oh my Dear God. What are they going to say?

CURTAIN

MISER, MISER!

A version of Molière's *L'Avare*

Translation
by Anthony Burgess

Characters

HARPAGON

ELISE, his daughter

CLEANTE, his son

VALERE

LA FLECHE, a servant

MASTER JACQUES, a cook and coachman

ANSELME

MARIANE

MAITRE SIMON

FROSINE

SERVANTS

The action takes place in Paris in the 1660s at the residence of an elderly miser named Harpagon.

Act One

Scene One

VALERE:

Elise, adored, delicious and well-loved

Elise – some nasty demon seems to have shoved

Or shovelled you into a gloomy pit

Or fit. Come, tell me what's the cause of it.

First you adorably tell me you return

The ardent love with which I bake and burn,

And now I see you sigh and sigh and sigh –

A very windy wet reply to my

Fire, a callous killjoy to my joy.

The things I meant were not meant to annoy.

You make me all delirious, then you seem

Repentant and regretful of the dream

We're going to make true, the fulfilment of

My love, your love, our one and mutual love.

ELISE:

Ah no, dearest Valère, I don't repent

One jot of all our amorous intent.

Its sweetness is so strong, but I am not.

I almost faint to think of it – ah, what

Joy... What makes me sigh? Well, this is it:

Happiness always breeds its opposite.

I'm afraid – afraid I love you overmuch.

VALERE:

Afraid? How can you be? My love is such

A flame. Your fear is ice in summer weather.

What do you fear?

ELISE: A hundred things together –

My father's anger – what the word will say.

Oh, but it's really this: I know the way

A man's mind works. The fire burns, then it's out.

Fear of that criminal coldness fans my doubt.

VALERE: Ah, no, Elise. Don't judge me like the rest.

I'm not like that. Most beautiful and best

Of girls, I swear to love you until death

Gives us the chop.

ELISE: It's just a puff of breath.

All men speak that way. Only actions show

The difference between them.

VALERE: You shall know,

My dearest, by a thousand million actions,

By all your needs and all my satisfactions,

The blazing bright sincerity of my passion.

So don't assassinate me in that fashion,

Bleeding me dry with treacherous incisions,

Seeking false crimes and making false previsions.

ELISE: An easy thing – to be persuaded of

The truth of love from someone that we love.

Valère, I do believe your heart, accept

Your deep-sworn vow. The nagging doubt that crept

Into my own is gone, is over, out.

VALERE: So tell me what the misery's about.

ELISE: I wouldn't have a thing to fan my sighs

If the world could but see you with my eyes.

Heaven itself, and daily memory

Tells me your virtues. Every hour I see

The bravery with which you rescued me

From – oh, you know; the deep devotion and

The love which made you leave your native land,

Your parents and your noble rank, and, rather

Than not see me, be a servant to my father –

Nobility in an ignoble dress:

This is enough, more than enough, to impress

The image of your love upon my heart,

But not enough, my dearest, to impart

Acceptance of our marriage to the world.

VALERE: My love and that alone has swirled and hurled

Me into this degradation. As for him,

Your father, father of your scruples, dim–

Sighted about everything but money –

Perhaps in a play this business would be funny:

Trying to match you up with anyone

Who seeks no dowry. Funny, but no fun.

Forgive me, dear Elise – not right I should

Talk to you like this. But it's not good,

This avarice, to say the very least.

I'd say he was an all-devouring beast

If beasts cared about money. But let it go.

Someday, somewhere, I'll find them both, I know –

Father and mother missing, God knows where.

I wait for news, but no news comes. I swear

I'll leave this job and find them –

ELISE: Dear Valère,

Don't move from here, I beg you. No, please rather

– Well, cultivate the good side of my father –

If you can find it.

VALERE: I do all I can,

Sustain the sweet complaisance that began

When I found service as your father's man,

Keep clean the mask of sympathy I wear

To give him pleasure and perhaps to tear

A little tenderness from his tough hide.

That is the only way – to seem to side

With all his prejudices, praise his vices,

Support him in some pennypinching crisis,

Applaud his foul philosophy – no matter:

Blame doesn't really lie with those who flatter

But those who must be flattered.

ELISE: If you tried

Perhaps to get my brother on our side –

VALERE: Difficult. The two are cheese and chalk,

            Him and your father. Difficult to talk

            One way to this and one way to the other.

            But you could use the love you bear your brother

            To angle for support. Though you mustn't say

            A thing until the hour or week or day

            Seems to you propitious. He's here! You stay.

            Very good, madame. I'm on my way.

ELISE: I don't think that I'd have the courage.

Scene Two

CLEANTE: Dear

            Sister, sister, thank the Lord you're here,

            Here and alone. I've something for your ear

            And your ear only. A secret I can't smother

            A second longer –

ELISE: Tell me then, dear brother.

            What is it?

CLEANTE: A million things in the cover of

            One single word. I'm in love.

ELISE: In love?

CLEANTE: In love.

            And that's all I dare say. The dutiful son

            I have to be, dependent (God!) on one

            Who'd squash and quash and quell – But even so

This love burns on my brow with such a glow

Nothing can put it out. So please don't start

Throwing cold water on a blazing heart

By saying it's impossible.

ELISE: Engaged,

Are you?

CLEANTE: Engaged — how can I be? Encaged —

That's more like it — imprisoned behind gold bars

That are no prison. Engrossed up in the stars,

This love. So don't dissuade me from it.

ELISE: Would I

Even attempt it? Come, you know me. Could I?

CLEANTE: No, sister, but you don't know what love is.

You've never felt its sweet asperities,

The precious agonies it can devise.

I fear your wisdom.

ELISE: Oh, I'm not so wise.

It only happens once. Or so I'm told.

Or so I know. If I should be so bold

As open up *my* heart. I think you'd find

I don't have that much wisdom in my mind.

CLEANTE: Can it be possible that you — ?

ELISE: Let's have your story

First. Who is she?

CLEANTE: Ah, the shimmering glory

Of her hair, her skin, her smile – Well, she's a young

Lady who's not being living very long

Just round the corner. Lovely. Oh, the warm

Glow of her presence, beauty of her form.

I was transformed into a different man

The moment I first saw her. Mariane –

That's her name. She lives with her poor mother,

A decent lady, always ill. No other

Care in the world except to care for her

Has Mariane, her gracious servitor.

Such grace, such goodness – ah, if only you

Could see her –

ELISE: Borrowing your point of view

I see enough already. If you love her,

More than enough.

CLEANTE: It's painful to discover

How poor they are. So marvellous it would be

To raise them in the world. But look at me –

Impotent –

ELISE: Impotent?

CLEANTE: To improve their lot,

Considering the father that we've got,

The miserly old –

ELISE: Yes, I can see what

Chagrin –

CLEANTE: See it? Live it. Both of us do.

The wretched life imposed on me and you –

Pinching and scraping – that old skinflint who

Forces me into debt in order to

Dress reasonably. Look – I had to tell you this:

I need your help. The snake will rear and hiss

When he hears both our stories. Yours, if you like,

You can tell me now. He'll bare his fangs and strike,

But, with the concerted effort that we make,

Well, maybe we can both defang the snake,

Unvenom him with the force of our sentiments.

And if not – well, for me the way lies hence

– Borrowing, borrowing and not paying back,

Eloping. And you too must tread the track

That leads to penurious heaven. We've endured

His tyranny too long. So be assured

My mind's made up.

ELISE: This purgatory started

When our poor mother perished broken-hearted

To find he had no heart.

CLEANTE: I hear his voice.

Let's go and steel each other in the choice

We have to make. For, one way or the other,

We'll win.

ELISE: I lack your confidence, dear brother.

130

Scene Three

HARPAGON: Bright and early –

LA FLECHE: Early anyway.

HARPAGON: Breathing the morning air.

LA FLECHE: Which costs nothing.

HARPAGON: Hey, you – off. Defiling my premises. Jail-meat. Gibbet-fodder. March.

LA FLECHE: Never seen anybody like him. A broken-down lodging for the devil himself.

HARPAGON: What's that you're hissing between your teeth?

LA FLECHE: Who gives you the orders to give me the orders –

HARPAGON: What?

LA FLECHE: To march?

HARPAGON: Want to argue, eh? Well, here's an argument. Off, quick, and out. Or I chop you.

LA FLECHE: What am I supposed to have done?

HARPAGON: What you've done is to make me highly desirous of not having you here. Off.

LA FLECHE: My master – your son – he told me to wait. On this spot.

HARPAGON: Go and wait in the street. I don't want you stuck on my premises like a post or a peg or a picket, taking in everything that goes on and taking advantage of taking it in. I don't want a dirty spy spying treacherously on my business. Look at those eyes – eating up every blessed thing I've got, looking all over the place to see what there is to steal.

LA FLECHE: How the hell could anybody do any pinching? You're not a pinchable man, are you? – what with keeping everything shut up ten times over and prowling round on sentry-go all the blessed day and night.

HARPAGON: I'll lock up what I want to lock up and do what guard duty I think fit to do. Got it? Spies and blabbers. And you're one of the ones that blab about why and when and where I keep my cash cached.

LA FLECHE: Got money hidden away round here, have you?

HARPAGON: I didn't say that. I said nothing about that, did I, cackhead? *(aside)* He gets me mad. He's one of the ones. *(To* **LA FLИCHE.***)* You're one of the ones, aren't you? Telling everybody about it.

LA FLECHE: What does it matter to me what you've got or what you've not got? Broad as it's long so far as I'm concerned.

HARPAGON: Oh, very philosophical. I'll give you two lots of philosophy, one for each earhole. *(He raises his hand.)* Go on – off.

LA FLECHE: All right. I'm off.

HARPAGON: Wait. You've got something there, haven't you?

LA FLECHE: Got? Me? What?

HARPAGON: Come here, let me look. Show me your hands.

LA FLECHE: There.

HARPAGON: The others.

LA FLECHE: Others?

HARPAGON: Others.

LA FLECHE: Keep extra ones in reserve, do I?

HARPAGON: You've got something in there.

LA FLECHE: Look for yourself.

HARPAGON: Plenty of room in those boots.

LA FLECHE: If ever a man deserved to be right to get like that – It makes it a kind of duty to be a thief.

HARPAGON: What was that?

LA FLECHE: What?

HARPAGON: You said something about being a thief.

LA FLECHE: I said: have a good rummage and then you'll know I'm not a thief.

HARPAGON: Just what I'm going to do.

(He rummages in **LA FLИCHE***'s pockets.)*

LA FLECHE: To hell with all misers.

HARPAGON: What was that?

LA FLECHE: What was what?

HARPAGON: You said something about misers.

LA FLECHE: That's right. I said to hell with them.

HARPAGON: And who were you talking about?

LA FLECHE: Misers.

HARPAGON: And who are these misers?

LA FLECHE: A kind of bad people that you see around.

HARPAGON: And who particularly did you have in mind?

LA FLECHE: What are you getting riled about?

HARPAGON: I'm getting riled because there's a good reason for getting riled.

LA FLECHE: You think I meant you?

HARPAGON: I'll think what I want to think. Saying that to me, were you?

LA FLECHE: I was saying it to my hat here.

HARPAGON: And I'll say something to a portion of your anatomy that doesn't wear a hat.

LA FLECHE: So I mustn't say to hell with misers?

HARPAGON: You mustn't say anything. I won't have your insolence.

LA FLECHE: I didn't mention anybody's name.

HARPAGON: Speak one word more and you know what you'll get.

LA FLECHE: When your nose is snotty – wipe it.

HARPAGON: Are you going to shut up?

LA FLECHE: In spite of my better judgment and my rights as a free citizen – yes.

HARPAGON: Haha.

LA FLECHE: By the way, you missed this pocket. Have a feel.

HARPAGON: I'm sick of rummaging. Hand it over.

LA FLECHE: Hand over what?

HARPAGON: What you took.

LA FLECHE: I took nothing.

HARPAGON: Sure?

LA FLECHE: Sure I'm sure.

HARPAGON: Get off then. To hell with you.

LA FLECHE: And the misers. *(He goes.)*

HARPAGON: Eh? Well, I've made him think twice anyway. Jailmeat and gibbet-fodder. Pig of a son's servant. I'll watch him.

Scene Four

HARPAGON: The trouble a man has just to look after his own. Still, that's what a man has to do, just keeping a little bit on one side for expenses. A difficult job – finding just one place in a man's house where he can be sure he's got it safe. Strong boxes – I don't trust them. An invitation to thieves, the first thing a thief goes for. I'm still not sure whether I've done the right thing – digging a hole in the garden to bury the ten thousand ĕcus I got yesterday. Ten thousand ĕcus – that's a hundred thousand pounds – real pounds, old ones, gold ones.

His son and daughter appear, talking together in low voices.

Oh dear God – I got carried away. Talked too loud. It's a bad sign when a man starts talking to himself. What is it?

CLEANTE: Nothing, father.

HARPAGON: How long were you there?

ELISE: We've only just got here.

HARPAGON: Did you hear anything?

CLEANTE: What, father?

HARPAGON: Just now?

ELISE: What?

HARPAGON: What I was just saying?

CLEANTE: No.

HARPAGON: All right then.

ELISE: Excuse me, father –

HARPAGON: I can see from your faces you heard what I was saying just then. I was just telling myself what a job it is to get hold of money nowadays. I was saying that a man would be lucky to lay his hands on a hundred thousand. In gold.

CLEANTE: We kept out of the way. We thought we might be interrupting something.

HARPAGON: Glad to hear you say it. Otherwise you might have heard something and got it all wrong – I mean, something like me saying that I'd got a hundred thousand – in gold.

CLEANTE: We keep out of your affairs, father.

HARPAGON: I only wish to God I had a hundred thousand. In gold.

CLEANTE: I didn't think you –

HARPAGON: It would be a fine thing, by God it would.

ELISE: There are some things –

HARPAGON: I could certainly do with it.

CLEANTE: I think –

HARPAGON: I'd be well away.

ELISE: Father, you're –

HARPAGON: And I'd not complain any more about times being bad. As I have to do all the time now.

CLEANTE: My God, father, you've no cause to complain. Everybody knows you're well off.

HARPAGON: Me? Me well off? They're all liars who say that. Liars and idiots. It's a damned falsehood, a bare-faced untruth.

ELISE: No need to be angry, father.

HARPAGON: So. My own children turn against me. My own flesh and blood – traitors and enemies.

CLEANTE: Am I your enemy, just for saying you're well off?

HARPAGON: Ah yes. Talk like that and the expense you put me to – one of these days somebody's going to come and cut my throat – strike me dead because he thinks I've got a fortune stashed away.

CLEANTE: You mentioned expense. What expense do I put you to?

HARPAGON: What expense? It's a damned crying scandal the way you show yourself off in the city – ribbons and laces and servants –

CLEANTE: Servant.

HARPAGON: I had a word with your sister here yesterday about her folderols. But you're worse. Much worse. It cries to heaven for vengeance to see you done up from head to foot – enough money there to invest at a fair interest. I've told you twenty times you're an absolute and utter disgrace to your father – got up like a marquis, and it all comes of robbing me and getting me ready for the poorhouse.

CLEANTE: Robbing you?

HARPAGON: How else do you explain the way you doll yourself up?

CLEANTE: Gambling, father, if you must know. Playing the tables. And when I'm lucky I put my winnings on my back.

HARPAGON: It's all wrong. If you're lucky at cards you should invest the cash at a decent interest. Look at you – what's the good of being done up like that – ribbons from head to foot, and those things hanging down on your topboots. Got to spend good money on wigs, have you, when your own hair's good enough, and that costs nothing. I reckon that in ribbons and laces and wigs you've got on your person at this moment anything up to twenty pistoles – one pistole is eleven pounds – in gold – and that adds up to two hundred and twenty – put out at interest that would bring in – let me see now – eighteen pounds six shillings and eight pence – every year!

CLEANTE: I suppose you're right.

HARPAGON: Leave it. Let it go. For the moment. There are other things to talk about. For the moment. What's the matter with you two? You look as though you're making signs to each other – which one of you is going to attack my coffers first. What do you mean by this fiddling about?

ELISE: We were deciding which one of us ought to speak first. We both have something to say to you.

HARPAGON: And I've got something to say to you – both of you.

CLEANTE: It's marriage we want to talk about. Marriage, father.

HARPAGON: Remarkable. And it's marriage that I have to talk about too.

ELISE: Marriage, father?

HARPAGON: Why this cry like a wounded stickleback? What is it makes you scared, my girl – the word or the thing?

CLEANTE: Marriage is something that frightens us both, father –at least, the way you're going to take it when we talk of it. I don't think we're going to see – well, eye to eye.

HARPAGON: Patience, my boy, a little patience. Nothing to be alarmed about. And you won't have any cause to complain about what I have in mind. Let's start from the bottom. Have you, by any chance, cast eyes on a young person named Mariane, who lives not very far from here?

CLEANTE: Why – yes, father.

HARPAGON: And you?

ELISE: I've heard about her.

HARPAGON: And what do you think of her, my son?

CLEANTE: A young lady of exceptional charm.

HARPAGON: Her – shall we say – physiognomy?

CLEANTE: Lively, sincere –

HARPAGON: Her general – ha – comportment?

CLEANTE: Altogether admirable.

HARPAGON: Would it be your view that a girl like that altogether deserves what any decent person of character would consider her to deserve?

CLEANTE: Well, yes.

HARPAGON: A desirable match, in other words?

CLEANTE: Well, yes – desirable.

HARPAGON: She has the qualities that would procure her a desirable match?

CLEANTE: Without any doubt.

HARPAGON: And that would totally satisfy any prospective husband?

CLEANTE: Assuredly.

HARPAGON: There's only one little difficulty. She isn't as well endowed with the world's goods as would seem, to the same prospective husband, altogether desirable.

CLEANTE: Oh, father, that's not in the least important. Her other qualities far outweigh –

HARPAGON: Pardon me, pardon me – what you seem to be saying is that what's lacking in worldly goods is compensated by – shall we say intangible ones?

CLEANTE: One way of putting it.

HARPAGON: Well, I'm delighted that we see eye to eye. Because it's precisely these intangible qualities that have captivated my heart. I've decided to marry her, provided, of course, that the tangible element isn't altogether missing –

CLEANTE: What?

HARPAGON: I beg your pardon?

CLEANTE: You've decided –

HARPAGON: To marry Mariane.

CLEANTE: You? *You?*

HARPAGON: Yes, me, me, me. I. What does that YOU mean?

CLEANTE: It's a bit of a shock, that's all. I'd better – Excuse me –

HARPAGON: Bit of a shock, eh? Go to the kitchen and treat yourself to a good big glass of cold water. These jackanapes, these young rips – they haven't the guts of a farmyard chicken. Anyway, daughter, that's my situation. As for your brother, I have a nice little widow in mind for him. And you – you're going to marry a certain Signor Anselm.

ELISE: Signor Anselm?

HARPAGON: That's right. A mature gentleman, very wise, very discreet, very well off. And he's not much more than fifty.

ELISE: *(with a curtsey)* Dear father, if you please – I have no desire to marry.

HARPAGON: *(with a bow)* Dear little daughter, if you please – I have every desire that you marry.

ELISE: I'm sorry, father.

HARPAGON: I'm sorry, daughter.

ELISE: I express my humble gratitude to Signor Anselm for his kind condescension, but, with your permission, I regret I am unable to marry him.

HARPAGON: I express my humble devotion to your ladyship, but, with your permission, you will marry him this very evening.

ELISE: This evening?

HARPAGON: This very evening.

ELISE: I fear not.

HARPAGON: I fear so.

ELISE: No.

HARPAGON: Yes.

ELISE: I say again – no.

HARPAGON: And I say again – yes.

ELISE: You will not reduce me to that humiliation.

HARPAGON: Humiliation or not, you will be reduced to it.

ELISE: I'll kill myself before I marry a man like that.

HARPAGON: You won't kill yourself. You'll marry him instead. Has anyone ever seen such insolence? Has any daughter ever spoken to her loving father in that manner?

ELISE: Has any father ever proposed such a marriage for a daughter?

HARPAGON: The decision is made; no more objections or unfilial contradictions. This is a match the whole world will approve of.

ELISE: This is a mismatch the whole world will condemn – if it has any sense.

HARPAGON: Ah – here comes Valère. Perhaps you would be good enough to allow him to make a judgment?

ELISE: I consent.

HARPAGON: Consent to abide by it?

ELISE: I will agree to whatever he says.

HARPAGON: Good; that's it then.

Scene Five

HARPAGON: Here, Valère. We have chosen you to decide between my daughter and myself on a matter of some importance. Who is right – that is the question – she or I?

VALERE: Oh, you, sir, no doubt at all.

HARPAGON: But do you know what we're talking about?

VALERE: No, but no matter. You're always right, sir – that stands to reason.

HARPAGON: This evening I intend to give my daughter's hand in marriage to a rich and respectable gentleman. And this idiotic little madam refuses the honour. What do you say to that?

VALERE: What do I say, sir?

HARPAGON: What do you say?

VALERE: Well –

HARPAGON: Yes?

VALERE: I say that – fundamentally – quintessentially, so to speak – you, of course, are absolutely right. But she – fundamentally, quintessentially – is not entirely wrong.

HARPAGON: What? Signor Anselm is a very considerable match – a gentleman of great nobility, wise, discreet, of exquisite manners and bearing and very well off. Moreover, he has no offspring by his first marriage. Could she conceivably do better?

VALERE: All you say is true. But your daughter might justly object that all this is somewhat precipitate – there is a need for a decent measure of time so that she can more gracefully adjust herself to the proposal –

HARPAGON: It's got to be done right away. There's a considerable advantage to this match that I haven't yet mentioned. He's willing to take her without a dowry.

VALERE: No dowry?

HARPAGON: No dowry.

VALERE: Ah – well – what can I say? You see? This should carry total conviction. Madame must – yield.

HARPAGON: It's a devil of a saving.

VALERE: Absolutely – no possibility of contradiction. Even though to your daughter this question of marriage presents a situation of immense significance to her future. Will she be happy or will she not? And this applies to the whole of her life. It is dangerous to undertake – at least not without the maximum of precautions – a venture whose outcome lasts till – well, death.

HARPAGON: No dowry.

VALERE: You're right, yes. That makes all the difference. There are, of course, people who might speak to you of the rights of the proposed bride – of her feelings, so to say –and of the undoubted inequality of age, feelings, temperament. Incompatibilities can wreck a marriage.

HARPAGON: No dowry.

VALERE: I can find no response to that. What possible contradiction could there be? What counter-argument could conceivably prevail? It's not just a question of raising the totally theoretical proposition that some fathers might be prepared to consult their daughter's happiness before their own financial advantage, would not be prepared to sacrifice the one to the other, and who would consider as possessing a certain not inconsiderable importance the whole question of marital harmony, joy, tranquillity, and all the rest of –

HARPAGON: No dowry.

VALERE: True, true. That shuts everybody's mouth. No dowry. A totally irrefutable argument.

HARPAGON: *(looking towards the garden)* Yes – I thought I heard a dog barking. Somebody there. Somebody after – you know what. Don't go away – I'll be back in a minute.

ELISE: Making a joke of it, are you, Valère, talking like that?

VALERE: I did it so as not to anger him.

I know the situation's pretty grim,

But contradiction would erode my plan.

Your father is a tough and stubborn man.

Some natures need a lateral approach.

If you confront them head on, try to broach

Your argument direct, they start to race

Along the road of rank unreason. Face

The fools and you're unfaced. Seem to consent

Even to a diabolic argument

And you can work angelic reason in.

To seem to lose – that is one way to win.

ELISE: But this marriage, Valère?

VALERE: I'll find a way –

ELISE: It's this evening.

VALERE: We'll get it put off somehow. You'll have to pretend to be ill.

ELISE: But he'll bring doctors in and they'll find out that I'm not.

VALERE: Are you joking? What do doctors know

Except how to be paid? Even if you show

The signs of ruddy health and say you're sick,

They'll name an illness for you double quick.

HARPAGON: Nobody there, thank God.

VALERE: If that won't work and there's no other hope

The only thing to do is to elope.

Say that you love me – say you love me still.

Here he is. As I was saying, a father's will

exacts obedience. If a husband's chosen for her – so be it. No dowry – that's the ineluctable argument. And if she can't see it, so much the worse for her.

HARPAGON: Well said. Perfectly put.

VALERE: I beg your pardon, sir. If you consider that I've spoken beyond my station and – er – laid it on a little.

HARPAGON: No, no, I'm delighted. And I leave it to you to drive the last remnants of unreason out of her. *(To* **ELISE**.*)* You, girl, you can't get away from it now. I grant him the authority over you that God grants me, and you'd better do precisely what he says.

VALERE: She still may try to resist, sir. With your permission, I'll follow her and continue the lessons I started.

HARPAGON: Do, do.

VALERE: Keep the bridle tight, so to speak.

HARPAGON: True, very true.

VALERE: So don't worry, sir. Everything will work out all right.

HARPAGON: Carry on, carry on. I'm going to take a little stroll. We'll see how she is when I get back.

VALERE: Money, sir, is the most precious thing in the world. And you must render humble thanks to your Creator that you are the honest man and exemplary father that you are. If I may say so. He gives life and he knows the purpose of life. When a gentleman proposes to take a bride *without dowry* – the fundamental and quintessential bounty of the Lord is revealed. Everything is contained in that expression. *Without dowry* – it usurps the place of all the virtues – youth and high birth, honour, wisdom, probity.

HARPAGON: An admirable lad. He spoke like an oracle. What happiness to possess a servant of that calibre. What happiness.

End of Act One

Act Two

Scene One

CLEANTE:	So there you are, you villain. Where've you been?
	What devilry has knocked and been let in?
	Didn't I say – in words of one syllable too –
LA FLECHE:	I know, I know, sir. I did what you told me to do –
	Planted my feet here like a pair of flowers,
	But then your father – up, out, at all hours –
	Glowers and growls and tells me to move on,
	Threatening and hitting. Go, he says. And I'm gone.
CLEANTE:	All right, all right. Tell me how things are going,
	Our little affair. The situation's growing
	More urgent. There's a thing you don't know of –
	My father (God!) has become my rival in love.
LA FLECHE:	In love? Your father?
CLEANTE:	Yes, and it was hell
	To hide my fury, wretchedness, as well
	As pure astonishment –
LA FLECHE:	In love? Him? Romeo?
	Him? Love? I never thought he'd even know,
	You know, the word. Love – it wasn't invented
	For his type, was it?
CLEANTE:	Kind fate has presented
	This new event to chide me for my crimes.

	Love has to choose this one time of all times
	To fuddle his brain. And love for my love too.
LA FLECHE:	You could have told him straight. Have said that you
	Were in love. With her. Why make a mystery?
CLEANTE:	Once he starts peering into my present history
	I'm lost, my plans are ruined. I had to choose
	The way of temporary silence. What's the news
	About our little venture?
LA FLECHE:	I tell you, sir,
	Once you get into the claws of a usurer
	You're done.
CLEANTE:	So, nothing doing?
LA FLECHE:	Pardon me,
	I didn't say that. Now, you know that we
	Have got this go-between called Master Simon.
	Pig as he is, he's spent a lot of time on
	This business – he says he likes your looks – he's let it
	Take up a lot of his working day –
CLEANTE:	Do I get it?
	The fifteen thousand?
LA FLECHE:	Yes, but upon conditions
	Laid down here. When you borrow, the position's
	Never straightforward.
CLEANTE:	Did he tell you who
	It's coming from?

LA FLECHE: Ah, what these gentry do

Is always a little devious. He won't say

His name, but he's arranged, sometime today,

A kind of conference. You must surrender

All possible personal details to the lender

About your family and the wealth they've got –

Property, cash, credit and whatnot.

It's always that way. No need to look queasy.

When they know who your father is, it should be easy.

Here are the articles the man dictated

Wherein the terms of borrowing are stated.

First, the borrower – over twenty-one;

The family whereof he is a son

Must possess ample property, free of debt,

And the financial status must be set

Down before a reliable notary

The lender will choose himself.

CLEANTE: So far, to me

That sounds acceptable.

LA FLECHE: The interest will be

Eighteen per cent.

CLEANTE: Eighteen per cent? Oh no.

There's fair dealing. But I shall have to go

Along with it.

LA FLECHE: This will take some digestion:

Unfortunately, the sizeable sum in question

Is not in the aforesaid lender's hands

And so, to meet the borrower's demands,

The lender must himself go to a lender

To meet the loan, obliging him to render

Interest of five per cent. Needless to say,

This sum the primary borrower must pay.

CLEANTE: Devil out of hell – a Shylock.

LA FLECHE: True.

Compliance or rejection's up to you.

There's something more. You wish to see it?

CLEANTE: No.

I need the money, so I'll have to go

Along with everything. What does it say?

LA FLECHE: This. The fifteen thousand that he'll pay

From goods whose price the lender estimates

At, naturally, favourable rates.

CLEANTE: What does that mean?

LA FLECHE: It's all been itemised.

First, a fourposter bed, wherein comprised

Are hangings, curtains, taffeta bedspread

In fine condition, coloured blue and red,

A canopy, of course, well-fringed in silk

And other fine accoutrements of that ilk.

CLEANTE: What would I do with that?

LA FLECHE:	God only knows.

Item: a painting tapestry that shows

A couple in an amatory pose.

Item: a walnut table with twelve legs

Whose rounded carpentry is smooth as eggs

But far less frangible, the item garnished

With panels for expansion, finely varnished.

CLEANTE: What in heaven's name –

LA FLECHE: Patience. I haven't done.

Item, three muskets, and on every one

Mother of pearl inset, triggers to match.

Item, a large brick furnace with attach-

Ments – pipes and tanks and funnels for refilling,

Useful for someone learned in distilling.

CLEANTE: I'll cut his throat –

LA FLECHE: He'll cut his own, God willing.

Item, a fine lute with its sonic spectrum

Of strings complete, along with a small plectrum.

Item, a set of draughts, finely encased,

To pass the time of those with time to waste.

Lastly, a lizard, stuffed, three feet or more

In length, to decorate a chamber floor.

All the above, being valued generously

At four thousand five hundred pounds, to be,

At the lender's discretion, assessed at three.

CLEANTE: May the plague rot him and his damned discretion –

             Hangman, may he hang –

LA FLECHE: I've the impression

             You're not too pleased.

CLEANTE: Swine – did you ever see

             So blatant a display of usury?

             He's not content with murderous interest

             But loads his rubbish on to me. At best

             I'd get five hundred on it. But, you see,

             He's got me in a corner: bastard, he

             Has bared his dagger, and it's at my throat.

LA FLECHE: You buy dear and sell cheap – a leaky boat

             But still you have to row it.

CLEANTE: Yes, and sink

             Before I get to shore. Why, do you think,

             Is parricide considered such a sin

             When fathers gloat at the mess their sons are in?

LA FLECHE: He's a man of the world: he wears his villainy

             Like a gold medallion. As for me,

             I've never had a powerful inclination

             To end up on the gallows. But temptation

             To risk it in a virtuous robbery

             – When I see him – sometimes comes over me.

CLEANTE: Give me that memorandum. Let me see;

             Though seeing's unbelieving –

Scene Two

MAITRE SIMON: To sum up, we

Have this young gentleman who needs money. His need is particularly pressing, so I've no doubt about his acceptance of all your conditions.

HARPAGON: Nothing at risk, then, Master Simon. You know his name, his family, his family's financial situation?

MAITRE SIMON: Well, not entirely. It just happened that I was approached about him by someone else. But he'll clarify everything himself, personally. His servant assured me that you'll be quite satisfied once you've got to know him. All I can tell you is that his family is exceedingly rich, that his mother's dead, and that he's prepared to undertake – for your personal satisfaction – that his father will be dead within, oh, eight months.

HARPAGON: Good enough. Christian charity, Master Simon – Christian charity obliges us to do all we can to help the unfortunate.

MAITRE SIMON: No doubt about that.

LA FLECHE: What's going on? Our Master Simon's having a word with your dear papa.

CLEANTE: Has somebody told him who I am? It wouldn't be you, would it?

MAITRE SIMON: Ah – urgency exhibits itself. You were informed about place and time? It wasn't myself, sir, who told them your identity and, ah, your place of dwelling. But there's no great harm in it. These are very discreet persons, sir, and you can explain the situation to them here and now.

HARPAGON: What?

MAITRE SIMON: This is the gentleman who wishes you to loan him the fifteen thousand pounds we were talking about.

HARPAGON: You! Villain! You've sunk down to this, have you?

CLEANTE: You! Father! You've sunk down to this, have you?

HARPAGON: It's you who want to ruin yourself with this damnable loan, is it?

CLEANTE: It's you who want to enrich yourself with this damnable usury, is it?

HARPAGON: How dare you show your face in my presence.

CLEANTE: How dare you show your face to the whole damned world.

HARPAGON: Have you no shame to sink to this level of debauchery, to bury yourself in a bottomless pit of impossible expense, to dissipate shamelessly the wealth amassed with sweat and pain by your long-suffering parents?

CLEANTE: Don't you blush to dig yourself into this bottomless pit of dishonour, to sacrifice honour and reputation in order to amass filthy money, and to indulge in the most infamous exertions of exaction ever contrived by the most criminal of usurers?

HARPAGON: Out of my sight, villain!

CLEANTE: Who, in your estimable opinion, is the bigger criminal – the one who buys the money he needs, or the one who steals what he doesn't need?

HARPAGON: I tell you to get out of my sight, or I'll make your two ears ring like bells. I'm not unhappy about this encounter. It's a warning, that's what it is, an injunction from holy heaven to keep an eye on your impudent villainies.

Scene Three

FROSINE: Sir.

HARPAGON: Just a minute. I'll be back. *(Aside.)* Time to take a look at you know what.

152

Scene Four

LA FLECHE: Droll, isn't it? He's got a place somewhere where he stores those bits and pieces on the list here. God knows what he's got. It would take some adding up.

FROSINE: Ah, you is it, poor little La Fluche? And what would you be after here?

LA FLECHE: Ah, you is it, Frosine? Same question.

FROSINE: Oh, you know, I have to be everywhere,

    Making myself useful here and there,

    Using the few talents that I've got

    To serve, to serve. That's life, is it not?

    Heaven gives wealth and rank to some. To me

    Nothing but hard work, tact –

LA FLECHE: And roguery.

    You've something on, then, with the old skinflint here?

FROSINE: A bit of business –

LA FLECHE: One word in your ear:

    You don't know Harpagon, not yet you don't.

    If you expect some cash from him you won't

    See a brass farthing.

FROSINE: But some services

    Have to pay well.

LA FLECHE: Listen, this skinflint is

    Of humans the most inhuman human yet,

    As hard a chunk of granite as you'll get.

Nothing you do for him will fetch a penny.

Gratitude? The swine has not got any.

Give is a word that's never pierced his head.

Give you good day – he lends it you instead.

FROSINE: I can milk men as other folk milk cows.

I've got my little skills. I can arouse

Their better feelings, tickle them inside.

I've never found a nag too hard to ride.

LA FLECHE: You'll never see a sou from Harpagon.

The man's a Turk, a really Turkish one.

You'll die ten deaths before he'll ever reach

Into his long pocket. He's a leech,

Leeching in cash, loving his money more

Than decent reputation. Ask him for

A farthing and he'll fall into a fit,

A frenzy – there's no other word for it.

A penny – that starts a consumptive cough.

You'll learn. You'll learn now. Here he is. I'm off.

HARPAGON: Everything in order. And what do you want?

FROSINE: By heaven, how well you look. A picture of health, strength, vigour –

HARPAGON: Who, me?

FROSINE: I'm never in my life seen such a fresh colour, so pink, so vibrant –

HARPAGON: Really?

FROSINE: Even when you were young you could never have looked as young as you look now. I've seen men of twenty-five who are ancient dodderers compared to you.

HARPAGON: Well, I'll never see sixty again.

FROSINE: Sixty? What's sixty? The flower of life. You're just about to enter a season of roses.

HARPAGON: Perhaps, perhaps. But I wouldn't mind being twenty years younger.

FROSINE: Are you joking? You have the complexion of a man who'll live to a hundred with no trouble at all.

HARPAGON: You think so?

FROSINE: Absolutely. You have all the signs. Don't move. There – between the eyes – the mark of long life.

HARPAGON: How do you know that?

FROSINE: Never mind. Let me see your hand. Heavens – what a life-line.

HARPAGON: Eh?

FROSINE: Just look how far it goes.

HARPAGON: And what does that mean?

FROSINE: All the way to the century – perhaps beyond – why not a hundred and twenty?

HARPAGON: That's not possible.

FROSINE: They'll have to put you to death – just to stop you from going on living. And there you are in the earth, long after your children and the children of your children.

HARPAGON: A pleasant idea. But leave it. How's our business going?

FROSINE: You have to ask? You honestly believe

That when I start a thing I don't achieve

An exquisite conclusion? As for marriage

My record's not besmirched by one miscarriage.

When I make matches they're just games of tennis.

I'd wed the Grand Turk to the Doge of Venice.

Your business is so sweet it's aromatic.

I told the mother and she's quite ecstatic

About your drawing up the contract now.

She made ten curtsies topped up with a bow

And said she'd be delighted to concur,

So don't expect a contretemps with her.

HARPAGON: Tonight I have to give supper to Signor Anselm. The girl ought to be there too. It saves expense.

FROSINE: Correct. The arrangement is that when she's dined

        (Lettuce and water, probably) she'll find

        Your daughter ready to accompany her

        To the fair – a sightseer, not a purchaser –

        The summer fair – you know, St Laurence's –

        This is the season, isn't it? It is.

        And when their brief non-spending trip is up, a–

        Rrangements are they'll both come here for supper.

HARPAGON: Oh well – I suppose they'll have to borrow my coach.

FROSINE: Up to you.

HARPAGON: But tell me, Frosine, have you spoken to the mother about the usual arrangement? The business side, so to speak?

FROSINE: Business. Didn't you know, didn't you hear

        She'll bring you in twelve thousand pounds a year.

HARPAGON: Twelve thousand?

156

FROSINE:	Yes. Their life's so economical,
	Frugality so extreme it could be comical.
	She's a girl who lives on salad, bits of cheese,
	Well-watered milk, sour apples, things like these.
	They keep a wretched table, and the girl's
	Never gone in for jewellery or pearls.
	There's a four thousand saving every year
	On clothes and furniture and suchlike gear.
	She goes in rags. And there's another matter:
	She's not a girl who likes to go and splatter
	Her cash about on cards. Just work it out –
	Five thousand pounds a year. You know about
	These women who waste millions upon gambling.
	Add four thousand for not liking rambling
	About in jeweller's shops or buying clothes.
	That's another nine. The dear girl loathes
	Expense of any kind. She'll fast, not feast.
	Doesn't that make another three at least?

HARPAGON: Not bad, not bad. But it's not real money.

FROSINE:	Pardon me. Isn't it really real,
	Sobriety, frugality and zeal
	For strict economy – all quite apart
	From loathing gambling with all her heart?

HARPAGON: It's a bit of an insult really, making a dowry out of something negative like that. I can't make up my accounts out of what I'm not spending, can I? I want something solid, solid.

FROSINE: By heaven, you'll have enough. Besides, they've got

               Some property overseas. You'll get the lot.

HARPAGON: Property overseas. How can I afford to travel to see if
    it's really there? Anyway, there's another thing. The girl's young,
    and the young go for the young. And I'm old, whatever you say.
    I foresee trouble in that department.

FROSINE: Ah! There's a thing I haven't told you of.

               The girl's so constituted she can't love

               Anyone young. She has to have old men.

HARPAGON: Men?

FROSINE: An old man. Haven't you heard that, then?

               There are such girls – gerontophiliacs,

               Who, when they see a young man, turn their backs

               But are quite ravished when they once have peered

               Upon a fine old codger with a beard.

               Older the better. Never go so far

               As to make out you're younger than you are.

               Sixty's her starting age and she'll unfix

               The contract if you say you're fifty-six

               And merely put your glasses on to sign it.

               She loves old noses and, to underline it,

               Prefers them to be decked with spectacles

               Even in bed. Young men are animals

               To her. She hates portraits of classic heroes

               Like Paris and Adonis. They're pure zeroes

               In her arithmetic. She rates far higher

Ancient Anchises rescued from the fire

Of Troy upon Aeneas's shoulders, Saturn,

Methuselah, and others of that pattern.

HARPAGON: Wonderful. I'd never have thought it. You know, if I'd been born a woman I don't think I'd ever have cared much for these youngsters.

FROSINE: You're right, of course. These pretty fly-by-nights,

What are they worth? They get involved in fights

To show their masculinity, strut and stride

Like peacocks – but there's nothing much inside.

HARPAGON: Yes, I don't know how women can lower themselves –

FROSINE: Lower themselves, yes, to embrace such nincompoops,

Mere chickens who'd be better off in coops.

There's nothing very lovable in youth,

Be youthful and you're useless – that's the truth.

HARPAGON: That's what I say all the time. Milkfed pullets, with their bits of moustaches like cat's whiskers, their wigs made of old rope, their topboots always falling down –

FROSINE: Compared with you, they've nothing much to blazon.

Here is a man it warms the heart to gaze on.

Dressed like a monarch, built like a marble tower,

Compact of dash and dignity and power.

HARPAGON: All right, am I?

FROSINE: All right? All wrong to libel you with faint

Praise of that order. Here's a face to paint.

Just turn a little. Walk a pace or two.

Look at that body. Nothing wrong with you.

HARPAGON: Nothing much wrong. A bit of bronchial trouble.

FROSINE: Bronchial trouble? That's no cause for grief.

                You can always spit into your handkerchief.

HARPAGON: Another thing. She's not seen me yet, has she? Not
noticed me passing by, for instance?

FROSINE: No. But I've done a verbal portrait of you.

                She knows that she'd be stupid not to love you.

HARPAGON: You've done well, and I'm grateful.

FROSINE: *(seriously)* If you could be so good as to demonstrate your
gratitude, sir, by helping me in a rather serious matter. A matter of
a lawsuit I'm bound to lose unless I can furnish a little of the ready.
You could be a source of supreme happiness to me if you'd only –

                (gaily)

                You can't conceive the joy that you will give her.

                The sight of you will pierce her to the liver

                With an erotic dart. She'll shake, she'll shiver

                When she sees you dressed up like this to kill.

                You'll make her mad for you, you really will.

HARPAGON: Thanks, thanks.

FROSINE: To tell you the truth, sir, this lawsuit looks like ruining me
unless I can get some help.

                I wish you could have seen her visage brightening

                At each new virtue that I listed. Lightning

                Struck from her eyes, pure incandescent pleasure.

                Her fingers writhed to clutch the promised treasure

                Of your combined perfections. Pale as the moon

                She cried: 'I must be married. Yes, and soon.'

HARPAGON: You give me great satisfaction, Frosine, and I'm greatly obliged to you.

FROSINE: I beg you, dear sir, give me the tiny morsel of help that I ask. That will put me back on my feet and I'll be eternally grateful.

HARPAGON: Goodbye now. I've some letters to write.

FROSINE: I assure you, sir, that you will never do me a greater service than in this that I ask.

HARPAGON: And, ah yes, I must make arrangements about the coach to take them to the fair.

FROSINE: I would never dream of importuning you like this if my necessity were not so great.

HARPAGON: And I'd better arrange to have supper fairly early. Better for the health that way.

FROSINE: I beg you not to refuse the small favour I ask. You have no conception, sir, of the benefit that would accrue from your assistance.

HARPAGON: Well, I must go. I think I heard somebody calling. We'll see each other sometime.

FROSINE: May the pox and the plague seize your villainous old carcass, dog and devil that you are. Deaf as a post when he wants to be, the wretched ingrate. But I'll have to push on with that business. I'll get paid for it if it's the last thing I do.

End of Act Two

Act Three

Scene One

HARPAGON: Come here, the lot of you. I'm going to give you your orders and tell you what your jobs are. You, Dame Claude, we'll start with you. Good, you've got your weapon at the slope. Clean up everywhere. And make sure you don't rub the furniture too hard – that's one way to wear it out. Now then, at supper I want you to be in charge of the bottles, and if you break one or slyly remove it, I'll take it out of your wages.

MASTER JACQUES: Such as they are.

HARPAGON: Off you go. You, Brindavoine, and you, La Merluche, I put you in charge of filling the glasses of the guests and giving them a drink, but only when they're thirsty. There are some impertinent lackeys who invite their master's guests to fill up and have another. Wait till somebody asks you for a glass, more than once, get that, more than once, and don't forget to mix plenty of water with it.

MASTER JACQUES: That's right. Wine neat goes straight to the head.

LA MERLUCHE: Do we have to stop doing our other jobs?

HARPAGON: Yes, but only when the guests arrive. And don't get your clothes dirty.

BRINDAVOINE: There's a big stain of lamp-oil on my only waistcoat.

LA MERLUCHE: I've got holes, pardon the word, in the bottom of my breeches. If anybody sees them, pardon the thought –

HARPAGON: Easy. Keep near the wall and always present yourself frontways. And you, hold your hat like this while you're serving. You, daughter, keep an eye on anything they do wrong and make sure there's nothing broken. That's the job of daughters. But now get yourself ready to receive my ah ah fiancře, who's going with you to see the fair, *see* the fair. You understand what I mean?

ELISE: Yes, father.

HARPAGON: And you, sir whippersnapper, I forgive you but of the goodness of my heart for your earlier behaviour. So let's see no more of that sour face and put a fair face on when you meet her.

CLEANTE: Me a sour face? Shove a sour face in hers? Why should I?

HARPAGON: Oh, we know how a man's children behave when a man remarries, how they look at the lady they're obliged to call stepmother. But if you wish to wipe out the bitter scalding memory of your early comportment, I recommend strongly that you smile sweetly and give her the heartiest welcome imaginable.

CLEANTE: To tell the truth, father, I can't promise to be altogether pleased about her becoming my stepmother. It would be a lie to say I could. But as for a warm welcome and a sweet smile, I can obey you absolutely in respect of that injunction.

HARPAGON: Make sure you do, then.

CLEANTE: You'll have nothing to complain about.

HARPAGON: Very wise, very wise. Valère, your assistance. Now then, Master Jacques, come here, I've kept you, till last.

JACQUES: Do you address me as your coachman, sir, or as your cook, me being both?

HARPAGON: The two together.

JACQUES: But which one first?

HARPAGON: Let's say cook.

JACQUES: A moment, please. *(He adjusts his appearance.)*

HARPAGON: What the devil ceremony is all that about?

JACQUES: Address your cook, sir.

HARPAGON: Right, Master Jacques. We have this supper tonight.

JACQUES: A miracle.

HARPAGON: Can you give us a good spread?

JACQUES: If you give me good money.

HARPAGON: Money, money, money, that's the only word I hear. Has nobody any other word in his vocabulary? Money, money, money. The one word in everybody's mouth: money. Always money. When they get up and when they go to bed – money. And in between too. Money.

VALERE: Impertinence, impertinence. It's the pride of a bad cook to spread the board with plenty of money. Easiest thing in the world and therefore detestable. It requires a man of spirit and ingenuity to do it with very little.

JACQUES: Big feed, small cash?

VALERE: As I said.

JACQUES: By the Lord, master steward, if that's what you now are, you'd oblige me greatly by taking over my job and revealing the great secret. Turn yourself into the general factotum while you're at it.

HARPAGON: Quiet. What do you think you need?

JACQUES: Your new head of the commissary here, he'll fill you to bursting on a couple of sous.

HARPAGON: Come on, tell me.

JACQUES: How many of you will there be?

HARPAGON: Eight or ten, I'm not sure yet. Say eight. If there's enough for eight, that's enough for ten.

VALERE: Or vice versa.

JACQUES: Well, you'll need four different kinds of soup and five other courses. Entrües, poulet, entremets –

HARPAGON: What the devil are you after – feeding the whole town?

JACQUES: A good roast –

HARPAGON: Still at it?

VALERE: Do you want to kill everybody off with overeating? Do you think the master here has invited these guests of his to stuff them to death? Go and read a guide to good health and ask the medical men if it isn't highly dangerous to gorge to excess.

HARPAGON: By God, he's right.

VALERE: Learn this, Master Jacques and all of your profession, that a table loaded with viands is an invitation to suicide, and the friendliest thing for a good host to do is to glory in the frugality of the dinner he gives. To quote an ancient saying: We must eat to live and not live to eat.

HARPAGON: Oh, that's beautiful. Oh, let me embrace you for that pearl of wisdom. It's the most wonderful phrase I ever heard in all my life. We must live to eat and not eat to live. No, it's not quite like that.

VALERE: The other way round.

HARPAGON: Who said it? What superlative brain was responsible for that gem of moral philosophy?

VALERE: His name escapes me.

HARPAGON: Don't let the words escape you. I want them written in letters of gold over the chimney in the dining-room. Well, let it look like gold.

VALERE: It shall be done. And as for this supper, kindly leave everything to me. Everything will be as it should be, sir.

HARPAGON: Get on with it, then.

JACQUES: You're welcome. Less trouble for me.

HARPAGON: We'll have things that people don't like much and at the same time fill them up. For the first course, of course. A fatty chunk of mutton with broad beans. A pвtŭ in a jar garnished with chestnuts. Plenty of those around in the garden.

VALERE: Leave it all to me.

HARPAGON: Now, Master Jacques, make sure the coach is cleaned out.

JACQUES: A moment. You're speaking to your coachman. *(He re-adjusts his dress.)* You were saying – ?

HARPAGON: Give it a good clean-out, and get the horses ready to pull it to the fair.

JACQUES: You speak of your horses, sir? They're not in a fit condition to pull anything. I won't go so far as to say that they're ready for the knacker's yard, not yet, but they're so thin, underfed, that they're more like ghosts of beasts, phantoms, ideas of horses in the mind of the devil.

HARPAGON: And if they're underfed, why not? They don't do anything to earn their fodder.

JACQUES: The poor creatures – it tears my heart out to see them look like skeletons. I love them, do you hear? I give them half-chewed scraps out of my own mouth to keep them going. It's not natural the way they are.

HARPAGON: Pulling a coach from here to the fair – that's not what I'd call heavy work.

JACQUES: Maybe not, but I haven't the heart to harness them, and it would go against my Christian conscience to give them a lick of the whip, what with the state they're in. How do you expect them to drag a coach when they've not the strength to drag themselves to their feet?

VALERE: Sir, I'll get Le Picard, you know, the man who lives next door, to drive them. And while we've got him he might as well help with the supper.

JACQUES: All right. I'd rather they died under somebody else's whip than under mine.

VALERE: Master Jacques bows to reason.

JACQUES: Master steward bows to necessity.

HARPAGON: Enough.

JACQUES: Sir, you know I don't go in for flattery, like some, and I can see well enough that his pinching grip on the domestic commodities – bread, salt, wine, candles and the rest – it's only to get in well with you. I get mad at that, I can tell you, and I'm sick of hearing what other people say about you. Because, to tell you the truth, I'm fond of you despite everything, and, next to my poor old nags, you're the animal that I love best in all the world.

HARPAGON: And what do they say about me?

JACQUES: You'll only get mad if I say.

HARPAGON: I never get mad.

JACQUES: Excuse me, I know damned well that what I say they say is going to make you mad all right.

HARPAGON: Ah no. I'll be delighted to hear.

JACQUES: All right, sir, if you want it that way, I'll tell you frankly and sincerely that they all have a laugh at you. Every day it's the same and from all quarters. They pick you up by the scruff of your arse, so to speak, and chuck you in the mud. Somebody says that you get special calendars printed so that you can double the days in Lent and make your people fast more. Somebody else says that you've always got a quarrel ready for the domestic staff at payday so they'll worry more about being thrown out than getting their wages. And then there's the story about you taking a neighbour's cat to court for eating a bit of your left-over scrag-end. And the other one about you getting up in the night to steal the horse's hay and your coachman – not me, the one you got rid of – bashing you with his stick and you not daring to say anything about it. I'm always hearing things like that. You're a legend in your own time and a laughing-stock. And the only names they call you by are: pennypinching villain, skinflint, usurer and bloody miser.

HARPAGON: *(Beating him.)* You're a villain yourself, as well as a fool and an impudent no-good.

JACQUES: Ah well. I guessed this would happen. You think it's all lies, but I knew you'd go mad if I told you the truth.

HARPAGON: Learn your manners, learn your place.

Scene Two

VALERE: That's what you get paid for plain speaking.

JACQUES: By God, master johnny-come-lately, the big man as he thinks himself to be, keep your snout out of it. Laugh when you get your own thumps with a stick but don't laugh at mine.

VALERE: No need to get riled.

JACQUES: *(aside)* Nicely, nicely. I'll lay it on a bit, and if he's fool enough to take it. I'll give him a taste. (aloud) Well, mister laugher, you don't see me laughing, do you, but if you get in my hair like that I'll make you laugh on the other side of your arse. (*He pushes him menacingly.*)

VALERE: Easy, easy.

JACQUES: Don't tell me easy. I take you hard.

VALERE: Come now –

JACQUES: Impertinent, that's what you are.

VALERE: Monsieur maotre Jacques –

JACQUES: Mister master, eh? Master mister. Laying it on a bit. Give me a stick and you'll see *me* lay it on.

VALERE: *I* don't need a stick. (*He pushes him back.*)

JACQUES: You're not supposed to do that.

VALERE: Now, mister master idiot, you'll see what I can do, and no supposing.

JACQUES: All right, you're making it clear enough.

VALERE: You're no more a cook than my fundament. Do you know that?

JACQUES: Yes, yes, agreed.

VALERE: You'll know what I am next time.

JACQUES: Sorry, sorry.

VALERE: Give me the big stick, will you?

JACQUES: I was only joking.

VALERE: Well, I don't like your jokes. *(Beating him.)* You're as bad a joker as a cook.

JACQUES: To hell with being sincere and honest. It doesn't work. No more telling the truth. The old bastard was right to lay it on. But I'll get my own back on this one, see if I don't.

Scene Three

FROSINE: Maotre Jacques, is your master at home?

JACQUES: He's at home. I know that well enough.

FROSINE: Tell him we're here, will you?

Scene Four

MARIANE:	I feel peculiar, Frosine, all bruised and bit.
	This meeting – I can't say I relish it.
FROSINE:	Why, what's the matter, what are you rattled at?
MARIANE:	Really, you have the nerve to ask me that?
	Imagine what a mare feels, newly snaffled,
	An innocent condemned who's shown the scaffold.
FROSINE:	Well, I agree, talking about the noose,
	Harpagon's not the gibbet that I'd choose,
	But that young man you spoke of – cast your eyes
	On him and you'll soon feel your spirits rise.
MARIANE:	This is another problem. I'm afraid
	The courteous little visits that he's paid
	Have touched my heart and fired my fantasies.
FROSINE:	But don't you know who the young fellow is?
MARIANE:	No, but I know that if I had my way
	I'd choose him for a husband any day,

	And that contributes to my lack of glee

And that contributes to my lack of glee

About the husband that they're giving me.

FROSINE: These young bloods are agreeable enough,

But most of them are rascally and rough.

It's best to be hitched up to some old codger

Even though you'd not have him as a lodger,

For after the marriage comes the funeral bell

And when he's dead you're free and rich as well.

MARIANE: It's a strange business, waiting for the day

Of someone's death so we can have our way

And live a little. But I've heard that wives

Who wish their husbands dead prolong their lives.

FROSINE: Ah no. You're only wedding this buffoon

In order to become a widow soon.

That's laid down in the contract. He has three

Months to live. If he lives longer, he

Is cheating.

MARIANE: Can we sue him?

FROSINE: Here he is

In person.

MARIANE: Oh, that ugly mug of his.

Scene Five

HARPAGON: Do not be offended, my little beauty, if I greet you wearing my spectacles. I recognise that your charms are visible enough without optic correction, and I don't need spectacles to observe them. But, after all, we use ground lenses to see the stars, and I consider you to be a star, and the most shining star in the starry firmament. Frosine, she doesn't speak a word, and I get the impression she's not overjoyed to see me.

170

FROSINE: It's a bit of a surprise, seeing you. And, as you know, young ladies don't like to exhibit their feelings at first blush.

HARPAGON: Yes, you're right there, I suppose. See, little darling, my daughter is here to greet you.

Scene Six

MARIANE: I'm afraid, madame. I've been slow in paying you a call.

ELISE: Madame, you've done what I should have done. I ought to have called on you first.

HARPAGON: Tall girl, isn't she? But rank weeds grow fastest.

MARIANE: *(To* FROSINE.*)* He's horrible.

HARPAGON: What says my beauty?

FROSINE: That you're h – h – admirable.

HARPAGON: You do me too much honour, my love.

MARIANE: He's beastly.

HARPAGON: Much obliged for your sentiments.

MARIANE: I can't go through with it.

HARPAGON: Here's my son to do you the honours.

MARIANE: Frosine, he's the one!

FROSINE: Marvellous coincidence, isn't it?

HARPAGON: I see you're astonished to see me with such grown-up children. But it won't be long before I'm rid of them, my dear.

Scene Seven

CLEANTE: An encounter, madame, I did not foresee,

A happy one. It's a surprise to me

My father had this marriage plan in mind.

MARIANE: I could say something of a similar kind.

                 This unforeseen encounter – so we find –

                 Is a surprise in common.

CLEANTE: I rejoice

                 In my astonishment. My father's choice

                 Could not have been a better one, but still

                 I must confess it goes against my will   .

                 To have you as my stepmother – a title

                 I find repugnant. I fear this short recital

                 Must smack to some here present of brash brutality,

                 And lack the flavour of polite formality,

                 But let me say this – with my sire's permission –

                 If I were in the fortunate position

                 Of regulating who should marry who,

                 I wouldn't let my father marry you.

HARPAGON: There's a fine impertinent compliment for you. There's
    a brilliant confession to make.

MARIANE: Well, all things being equal, I confess

                 That if that title causes you distress,

                 I wouldn't have you for a stepson either.

                 Please don't misunderstand me – only, by the

                 Profound inquietude you show me now

                 I'm forced to say I would revoke the vow

                 I'm forced to take if only it would serve

                 To cancel the chagrin that I observe.

HARPAGON: Well, she had to say that really. Right in a way. A stupidity is cancelled out by another stupidity. I apologise, my dear, for my son's impertinence. He's a young fool, and he's not yet learned how to weigh the consequences of his words.

MARIANE: I assure you, sir, I've taken no offence.

His sentiments betrayed a lot of sense.

I like such honesty, however grim.

If he'd said different, I'd think less of him.

HARPAGON: Too much kindness, my love, we'll soon knock that out of you. Time will change this one and you'll see him behave differently one of these days.

CLEANTE: Believe me, sir and madam, when I say

I'll never change, not till my dying day.

HARPAGON: Still at it, eh? More pigheaded than ever.

CLEANTE: You want me to betray the way I feel?

HARPAGON: Change your tune, lad, change it.

CLEANTE: Change it? We'll

Have a diverse discourse to please my father.

Madame, believe me when I say I'd rather

Be in his shoes than mine. And let me swear

I've never seen such beauty anywhere,

And can conceive of nothing equal to

The lifetime happiness of pleasing you,

To be your spouse must be a raging glory

Not to be read of in a fairy story,

And that felicity would raise me high

Higher than the Sun King shining on Versailles.

Ah yes, to usurp my father's blest position

Would be the very peak of my ambition.

There's nothing in the world I wouldn't do

If I could boast so sweet a conquest – you.

HARPAGON: Easy, son, easy.

CLEANTE: Just a little compliment.

HARPAGON: I've got a tongue, haven't I? I've no need of a procurer – a go-between, that is. Come, let's sit.

FROSINE: No, we must go to the fair. We'll get back all the earlier and have all the more time to chat.

HARPAGON: Get the coach. Get the horses. I beg you to forgive me, my beauty – I should have thought of giving you a little collation before you go.

CLEANTE: I saw about that, father. I bought on your behalf – you'll get the bill – a few dozen oranges, some sweet limes, and some boxes of candy.

HARPAGON: Valère!

VALERE: Out of his mind.

CLEANTE: Do you think that's enough, father? I hope madame will excuse its insufficiency.

MARIANE: Oh, too much.

CLEANTE: Have you ever seen a more brilliant stone than this diamond on my father's finger?

MARIANE: Lovely.

CLEANTE: *(Removing the ring.)* It's better close to.

MARIANE: Beautiful. All crystal and fire.

CLEANTE: For the loveliest hand in the world. A little gift from my father.

HARPAGON: From me? Who said?

CLEANTE: Isn't it true, father, that you wanted her to keep it? A token of love?

HARPAGON: What? What the devil do you think you're playing at?

CLEANTE: Very gracious. He asks me to insist that you accept it.

MARIANE: Oh, I couldn't.

HARPAGON: I'll go mad.

MARIANE: It's too much –

CLEANTE: You mustn't offend him. See, offence.

MARIANE: Well, thank you. But I can't.

CLEANTE: Not at all. You can.

HARPAGON: May all the pocky boils of St Anthony's fire light on you.

CLEANTE: See, he's still trying to get over your refusal.

HARPAGON: Villain, traitor.

CLEANTE: Desperation. But he's getting over it.

HARPAGON: Swine that you are.

CLEANTE: My fault, father. I try to make her keep it. But she's very obstinate.

HARPAGON: Jail-meat.

CLEANTE: Madame, you seem to be the cause of a family quarrel.

HARPAGON: Food for the gallows.

CLEANTE: You'll make him ill. Don't, I beg you, refuse any more.

FROSINE: Oh, what a fuss about nothing. Keep the ring, he wants you to.

MARIANE: Well, I wouldn't want to make him any angrier. All right.

Scene Eight

BRINDAVOINE: Sir, there's a man wants to speak with you.

HARPAGON: Tell him to come back some other time.

BRINDAVOINE: He says he's got some money for you.

HARPAGON: I beg his pardon. I'll be back.

Scene Nine

LA MERLUCHE: *(Running in, he makes* **HARPAGON** *trip.)* Oh, sir –

HARPAGON: Ah, I'm dead.

CLEANTE: What is it, father? Have you hurt yourself?

HARPAGON: That traitor's been given money by one of my debtors to make me break my neck.

VALERE: It doesn't seem to be anything.

LA MERLUCHE: Beg pardon, sir. I was just running in to tell you something quick.

HARPAGON: What is it, murderer?

LA MERLUCHE: To tell you that your two horses have lost their shoes.

HARPAGON: Send them to the blacksmith.

CLEANTE: While they're being re-shod, I'll do the honours of the house, father, take madame into the garden, and persuade her to eat heartily of our cold collation.

HARPAGON: Valère, keep an eye on them. Grab all you can before they scoff it.

VALERE: Naturally.

HARPAGON: Oh son, you damned accursed impertinent unfilial villain – do you want to ruin me?

End of Act Three

Act Four

Scene One

CLEANTE: Come back in here. There's nobody about,

And we can have our sad discussion out.

ELISE: Yes, my dear. I've been made a party to

The passion that my brother bears for you.

I know about the obstacles that make

True love lose heart and hearts quiver and quake

And I assure you that I'm much concerned

To see fulfilled the happiness you've earned.

MARIANE: It's a sweet consolation to be aware

That someone of your character should care

About my interests. Please let it continue,

This friendly generosity that's in you,

To mollify the cruelty of fortune.

FROSINE: You're mad, you know. Why didn't you importune

Someone like me to look at your affair?

I could have intrigued, burrowed here or there

And stopped this business being what it is.

CLEANTE: A matter of locked fates, blocked destinies.

Sweet Mariane, have you any ideas?

MARIANE: My state, alas, is just as it appears –

Dependent, impotent and negative.

There's not one word of counsel I can give.

I live in wishes.

CLEANTE: Nothing more than those

For hope to lean on? No point of repose

For my bruised feelings, no burst of affection,

No mirror that hurls back my love's reflection?

MARIANE: What can I say? Put yourself in my place,

Consider the big blank brick wall I face.

I leave it all to you. You are a man –

It's up to you to plan, do what you can.

Don't force me to express what isn't fit

For my enforced dependence to permit.

CLEANTE: Ah, scruples, honour, all the rest of it.

Obedience, promises – they make me –

MARIANE: What can I do? The constraints of my sex

Get in the way. I'd die rather than vex

My mother, who has brought me up with such

Tender affection. It would pain me overmuch

To give her pain. But you can work on her,

Gain her good graces, act as you prefer.

I grant you franchise. And if you wish it now –

A declaration, protestation, vow –

You have it.

CLEANTE: Darling! You, my poor Frosine,

Will you agree to help us?

FROSINE: I've not been

Considered wholly human or humane

– Which is the right word? – but it gives me pain

To think that people think I'm made of brass.

Of course I'll seek a way to overpass

This tangled traffic. What would you have me do?

CLEANTE: Just think a little.

MARIANE: Turn the light on.

ELISE: You

Can disentangle what you've helped to tangle.

FROSINE: Problems, problems. The maternal angle

Is not too difficult. Your mother's reasonable

And I don't think she'll find it at all treasonable

To shift love from the parent to the son.

But there's your real trouble. He's the one.

Your father is your father.

CLEANTE: All too true.

FROSINE: Various paths are open to the view.

To get your own way work upon his spite.

He'll let you have what seems to hurt you.

CLEANTE: Right.

FROSINE: Or Mariane could have a sort of rival.

A lady who could spark off the revival

Of lust for cash not beauty in a bride

That might well do it. Supposing that I tried

To get one of my friends to counterfeit

Someone of quality with a family seat

In Lower Britanny, a false marquise,

A lady of a certain age, who sees

How lovable he is.

CLEANTE: That would be funny.

FROSINE: Armed with a million pounds in ready money.

He says he loves you, Mariane, but get a

Bride like that and he will love her better.

CLEANTE: Well thought.

FROSINE: I'll do my best.

CLEANTE: And be assured

You'll have my gratitude as a reward.

I've nothing else.

FROSINE: I accept the recompense.

CLEANTE: My darling Mariane, you must commence

Gaining your mother's grace and confidence

With all the eloquence and charm and grace

Heaven – heaven bless it – has seen fit to place

In your sweet mouth and lovely eyes. Let's use

Your douce persuasiveness. She'll not refuse

To let the argument proceed until

We tie our knot.

MARIANE: I will.

CLEANTE: I know you will.

Scene Two

HARPAGON: Yes, yes, kissing the hand of his future stepmother and his future stepmother not saying no. Something's going on here.

ELISE: Here he is.

HARPAGON: The horses are shod and it cost a pretty penny. You can go off as soon as you like.

CLEANTE: Since you're not going with them, father, permit me to take your place.

HARPAGON: Ah no. Stay here. They'll be all right as they are. I need to have a word with you.

Scene Three

HARPAGON: Now then, leaving out the stepmother bit, how does she strike you?

CLEANTE: Strike me?

HARPAGON: Strike you – her general appearance, beauty, charm, that sort of thing.

CLEANTE: Well –

HARPAGON: Speak up.

CLEANTE: To be honest, she's not quite what I expected. Too much of the coquette about her. A bit gauche in her manners, not much beauty there, pretty mediocre all round. I'm not saying that to put you off. As a stepmother, I suppose I might as well have her as anybody else.

HARPAGON: The way you talked to her gave me a different impression.

CLEANTE: I piled on the compliments only to please you.

HARPAGON: Not because you rather fancied her yourself?

CLEANTE: Me? Never in this world.

HARPAGON: Pity. That rather puts paid to an idea that came to me when I was looking at you both together. I was thinking about, you know, my age. Whether it was convenient for me to be saddled with a girl as young as that. I thought of giving up the whole project and handing her over to you.

CLEANTE: To me?

HARPAGON: To you.

CLEANTE: Marry her?

HARPAGON: Marry her.

CLEANTE: Listen. She doesn't appeal to me a bit, but to please you I'd do anything. I'll take her.

HARPAGON: Please me? I'm not as unreasonable as you seem to think. I'd never force you.

CLEANTE: I'm not talking about force. I'm talking about giving you pleasure of my own free will.

HARPAGON: No, no, a marriage doesn't work out on those kind of terms. There has to be the inclination.

CLEANTE: That will come, father, in time. They say that love's not the root of marriage but the fruit of it.

HARPAGON: No, a man can't risk it. I've heard of terrible consequences to that sort of thing. If you'd shown any inclination to her. I'd have said marry the girl. But as you haven't, I'll go back to the old plan. I'll marry her myself.

CLEANTE: Very good, father, very good. If it's like that, I'd better open up and let a secret out. I love her. I've loved her from the day I first saw her. I had the intention of telling you about it, but then I was scared – scared of your response.

HARPAGON: Been visiting her, have you?

CLEANTE: Yes, I have.

HARPAGON: Often?

CLEANTE: Often enough, considering the time element.

HARPAGON: Received with open arms, were you?

CLEANTE: Well received, but they didn't know who I was, who I am. That was what gave such a shock to Mariane.

HARPAGON: You declared your love, as you'd call it, and talked about marriage?

CLEANTE: Yes. And I made the usual overtures to her mother.

HARPAGON: And she heard you out?

CLEANTE: Very civilly.

HARPAGON: And the girl ah ah reciprocates?

CLEANTE: If words and looks are anything to go by, I'd say yes.

HARPAGON: Well, you've let me in on your little secret and given me straight answers. And now, my son, you'd better start falling out of love as quick as you can. It's a disgrace for a son to court his own's father betrothed. As for getting married, that will be seen to for you, and very soon. I've got this widow lined up.

CLEANTE: Widow? How old? How ugly? I'm sick of your games. Since we've reached this pitch of sincerity, I tell you sincerely, frankly, and loudly, that I will not give up Mariane, not under any circumstances, and no matter what the strength of the opposition.

HARPAGON: How dare you have the audacity to speak so audaciously to your father! How dare you try to steal your father's property!

CLEANTE: Why yours more than mine? I saw her first.

HARPAGON: Am I not your father? Am I not entitled to deference and respect?

CLEANTE: There comes a time when deference is no longer decorous. Love laughs at filial duty.

HARPAGON: By God you'll learn what that duty is. I'll get my whip to you.

CLEANTE: Threats, threats, to the devil with your threats.

HARPAGON: You will give her up, puppy.

CLEANTE: Ah no.

HARPAGON: Where's my stick? You, fetch me a cat-o-nine-tails.

Scene Four

JACQUES: Gentlemen, gentlemen, what is this?

CLEANTE: I laugh in your ugly face.

JACQUES: Ah, please, sir, easy, easy.

HARPAGON: Impudence, you whelp, you –

CLEANTE: I won't give her up.

JACQUES: Speaking to your father like that!

HARPAGON: Leave him to me, the puppy dog.

JACQUES: Speaking to your son like that!

HARPAGON: If you want to interfere, interfere. Judge. See who's right.

JACQUES: Very good, sir. *(To* CLEANTE.*)* Move a little way off.

HARPAGON: I'm in love with a lady and I'm going to marry her. And this chunk of gallows-meat has the insolence to love her too and to go on doing it against my orders.

JACQUES: Terrible.

HARPAGON: Don't you consider this to be a ghastly crime, for a boy like that to cross his father in love. It's the crime of Oedipus or somebody like him.

JACQUES: Quite right. Stay there. Let me have a word with him.

CLEANTE: So you're to be the judge, are you? Well, you can be the court reporter instead. You can take a message to that old devil there.

JACQUES: Happy to be your messenger.

CLEANTE: I'm in love and that's that and that old idiot wants her too. Well, I won't have it.

JACQUES: You're right. I mean, he's wrong.

184

CLEANTE: Has he no shame, at his age, to talk about marrying? To pretend to be in love? And with a girl too young to be his daughter?

JACQUES: Right, right. I'll have a word with him. Sir, your son there is not so unreasonable as you seem to think. He says he's aware of the respect and duty he owes you and that he was carried away and he'll honour and obey if only you treat him a bit better and give him somebody in marriage that he can sincerely love.

HARPAGON: Ah. Tell him if he means what he says I'll hold nothing back from him and he can marry who he likes so long as it isn't Mariane.

JACQUES: *(To* CLÉANTE.*)* Right, your father is not being as unreasonable as you think he is, and he sees it's only the way you behave that makes him fly off the handle, and if you behave better you can marry who you like so long as you show him respect and deference and all the rest of it.

CLEANTE: All right, Master Jacques, tell him that if I can only marry Mariane he'll see in me the most submissive of sons, ready to do his bidding at the drop of a chapeau.

JACQUES: Everything's fine. He agrees to what you say.

HARPAGON: I ask nothing better.

JACQUES: It's all over, then. He abides by what you promise.

CLEANTE: Thank God for that.

JACQUES: Gentlemen, all's made up. Talk lovingly together. You were quarrelling without listening. But now you've listened to me you're in total agreement.

CLEANTE: Master Jacques, I'm obliged.

JACQUES: Nothing, nothing.

HARPAGON: You've done well, Master Jacques, and that deserves a little reward. Go off, I'll remember to give it.

He takes his handkerchief out of his pocket as if to give him a present.

JACQUES: I'll remember to thank you.

Scene Five

CLEANTE: I beg your pardon for my unforgivable behaviour.

HARPAGON: Nothing, nothing.

CLEANTE: I regret it more than anything in the world.

HARPAGON: For my part, I have all the joy in the world at seeing you recover your reason.

CLEANTE: How gracious of you to forgive my desperate fault.

HARPAGON: A father has no trouble in forgiving his children when they recover a sense of deference, duty, and love.

CLEANTE: No resentment?

HARPAGON: None at all.

CLEANTE: I assure you that till my dying day I'll preserve in my innermost heart the memory of your extreme generosity.

HARPAGON: And I assure you that there's no request of yours that I'll prove unwilling to grant. Within reason.

CLEANTE: Father, you've granted me all I ask. What more do I want but Mariane?

HARPAGON: What?

CLEANTE: You've made me ecstatically happy by your kindness in permitting me to take for my own my beloved Mariane.

HARPAGON: Who said you could do that?

CLEANTE: You did.

HARPAGON: Me?

CLEANTE: Unreservedly.

HARPAGON: What? But you just promised to give her up.

CLEANTE: Give her up? Me?

HARPAGON: That's right.

CLEANTE: Ah, no.

HARPAGON: You mean you won't give her up?

CLEANTE: I'm more resolved than ever.

HARPAGON: Villain. Traitor. Ingrate. Murderer.

CLEANTE: Nothing will change my resolve.

HARPAGON: We'll see about that, you damned Oedipus.

CLEANTE: Do what you please.

HARPAGON: Out of my sight. I don't want to see you.

CLEANTE: Very well. *Au revoir.*

HARPAGON: Never again. I have no son.

CLEANTE: So be it.

HARPAGON: I abandon you to the winds of heaven.

CLEANTE: Do that.

HARPAGON: I disinherit you.

CLEANTE: That is your privilege.

HARPAGON: And I give you a father's curse.

CLEANTE: You can keep your gifts.

Scene Six

LA FLECHE: *(Coming from the garden with a metal box.)* Sir, sir, look what I've found. Come with me quick.

CLEANTE: What is it?

LA FLECHE: Come, I tell you. Our troubles are over.

CLEANTE: What's going on?

LA FLECHE: I've been gloating over it all day.

CLEANTE: But what is it?

LA FLECHE: Your father's money – I've got it.

CLEANTE: How? How did you do it?

LA FLECHE: I'll tell you everything. Quick, out, away. I can hear him screaming his head off.

Scene Seven

HARPAGON: Thieves! Thieves! Murderers! Justice, justice, I call on heaven for justice! I'm ruined, lost, my throat's cut, they've robbed me of my life. Who did it? Who? Where? Where's he hiding? What can I do, oh God? How can I find it, them, him. Where can I run to? Who is it? Got you. Give me back my money, villain, wretch, assassin. Oh, it's me. I don't know what I am or where I am or who I am. I don't know what I'm doing, they've driven me mad. Oh, my poor money, my beloved, my only friend. I'm lost, I've lost – my love, my joy, my only salvation. The world's come to an end. It's doomsday. Finished, finished, done for. How can I live without my love? I can't, so I have to die, I'm dead, I'm buried. I can hear the organ play. Is there no one in the entire universe I can turn to, to restore me, to restore my love, my life? Eh? What's that you say? That's right, nobody. But who was it? When did he come? He chose the right moment for his deadly sin – when I was talking to my son from the deep, rejected, betrayed heart of a loving father. I'll have justice. I'll have an inquisition. Everybody – servants, son and daughter, me, mother – no, she's dead, she's in the clear. Everybody bears the mark of the Cain who was the first thief. No, the first murderer – but where's the difference? I can hear talk, somebody's talking. Saying how they did it, laughing, tearing my liver out, spitting on my entrails. By the Lord God, if anyone knows who it is, I'll go down on these old bones and supplicate, give everything I have. But they've taken everything. Is he down there? Are you hiding the sinful wretch? Everybody's looking at me, everybody's laughing. They all did it, they're all involved. A hundred-handed, thousand-handed thief. Quick, the police, judges, juries, state torturers, principalities and powers and common executioners. I'll hang the whole world by its neck. And if I don't get my darling back – I'll hang myself after.

End of Act Four

Act Five

Scene One

SUPERINTENDENT: Leave it to me. I know my job, thank the Lord. I know all about robberies. I wish I had as many thousand francs as I've hanged robbers.

HARPAGON: I've got all the magistrates of Paris dusting their wigs. If I can't get my money back I'll have justice, justice and justice.

SUPERINTENDENT: Very good. We must take our time in travelling all the roads of investigation. You said that you had in this box –

HARPAGON: A hundred thousand in gold.

SUPERINTENDENT: A hundred thou –

HARPAGON: A hundred – *(He breaks down.)*

SUPERINTENDENT: A considerable loss.

HARPAGON: There's no scaffold high enough to match the enormity of the crime. And if the criminal goes unpunished – nothing's safe, not the most sacred things in all the world are safe any more.

SUPERINTENDENT: In what denominations was this sum?

HARPAGON: Guineas, gold louis, doubloons, good solid heavy pieces that would weigh a man down.

SUPERINTENDENT: And have you your suspicions?

HARPAGON: Everybody. I suspect everybody. Arrest the lot, put the whole town on trial.

SUPERINTENDENT: We have to have our proofs, our testimonies. We must go softly softly.

Scene Two

JACQUES: I go and I come back. Let me have my throat cut, let my feet be grilled to a turn, let me be plunged in boiling water, let me be hanged from the rafters.

HARPAGON: Ah – confession, confession.

JACQUES: A matter of a sucking-pig, your honour, that big man chief steward johnny-come-lately of yours has had sent in for the supper.

HARPAGON: Forget pigs. This gentleman here has other things to ask you about.

SUPERINTENDENT: Don't be frightened. Sweetly and softly is my motto.

JACQUES: He's another one coming to supper?

SUPERINTENDENT: Here's you and here's your master. Have you something to tell him by any chance?

JACQUES: Tell him? Listen, sir, I do my job and I serve up what I'm paid to serve up.

HARPAGON: This is not the thing in question.

JACQUES: If I can't dish up what you have in mind, blame this steward you've got. Cheeseparing scissors. Economy. My hands are tied.

HARPAGON: Traitor, I'm not talking about the supper. I want news of the robbery. I've been robbed.

JACQUES: Had some money taken, have you?

HARPAGON: Yes, idiot. And you're going to hang high if you don't give it back instanter.

SUPERINTENDENT: Softly, gently. I can see from his face he's an honest man. No need to shove him in jail to get the truth from him. Yes, my friend, if you'll confess what you've done things will go easy for you under the rigour of the law. Some money's been taken from here today and you look like the sort of man who might know something about it.

JACQUES: *(aside)* Chance to get even. I'll nobble his favourite.

HARPAGON: What are you mumbling about?

SUPERINTENDENT: Leave him. He's an honest man and he's getting an honest statement ready.

JACQUES: Sir, your honour, if you want it straight, there's only one man with the gall to do it, and that's this new steward.

HARPAGON: Valère?

JACQUES: That's the one.

HARPAGON: Him? He? That paragon of fidelity and good service?

JACQUES: The same. He did it.

HARPAGON: And what makes you think so?

JACQUES: Think so?

HARPAGON: Think so.

JACQUES: Well, to my way of thinking he just did.

SUPERINTENDENT: Ground of suspicion? Proof?

HARPAGON: Did you see him prowling around the place where I'd put my money?

JACQUES: Oh yes. And where was it?

HARPAGON: In the garden there.

JACQUES: That's right. Prowling in the garden. So he was. What was this money in?

HARPAGON: A box.

JACQUES: That's it. He was prowling around with a box.

HARPAGON: What sort of a box?

JACQUES: Sort of a box?

HARPAGON: Of a box.

JACQUES: Well, you know – six sides, eight corners. In other words, a box.

SUPERINTENDENT: That makes sense. But be more explicit.

JACQUES: Split it? Oh, I see what you mean. Pretty big.

HARPAGON: Mine was little.

JACQUES: Well, in one way it was big and in another way little. That sort of depends.

SUPERINTENDENT: What colour was it?

JACQUES: Ah – you mean colour?

SUPERINTENDENT: Colour.

JACQUES: Oh, there was a colour all right. Has to be, hasn't there? Red, would it be?

HARPAGON: No, grey.

JACQUES: Reddish-grey or greyish-red, one or the other. That's what I was trying to tell you.

HARPAGON: That's the one. Write down the deposition. Oh, who can I trust any more? You can't swear by anyone. I'll end up robbing myself.

JACQUES: Here he is now. Don't tell him what I've told you.

Scene Three

HARPAGON: Come here. Confess. Confess the blackest crime, the most horrible sin that's ever yet been committed. Go on, start.

VALERE: I don't understand.

HARPAGON: Traitor and hypocrite, why don't you blush with the fire of your hellish crime?

VALERE: What crime are you talking about?

HARPAGON: As if you didn't know. Don't try to brazen it out, infamous wretched traitor. You've been found out, we know everything. How could you take advantage of my goodness? Smarming and smiling and saying yes yes yes and then to do a trick like that.

VALERE: Well, sir, if I've been found out, I won't waste time in denying the crime, as you call it.

JACQUES: So – I got it right without thinking.

VALERE: It was my intention to tell you about it, but it was always a question of waiting for a favourable moment that never arrived. But now the time seems to have come, I entreat you not to give way to anger while I tell how and why –

HARPAGON: So give me your how and why, you damned thief.

VALERE: Damned thief? This is hardly a name I merit. It's true that I've committed an offence against you, but surely, as you'll see, it's a pardonable one.

HARPAGON: Pardonable! Pardonable! He calls assassination pardonable!

VALERE: Please temper your anger. When you've heard me out, you'll admit that the crime or fault or indiscretion is not as heinous as you think.

HARPAGON: He calls it an indiscretion. You jailbait, to rake my entrails, drink my blood –

VALERE: Your blood is not being dishonoured. My social condition ensures that, though you know nothing about it yet. It ensures also a total capacity to make good what I did, if I did, wrong.

HARPAGON: Wrong wrong wrong. I'll have back what's mine, you blood-sucking-pig, instanter.

VALERE: Your honour, sir, will be thoroughly satisfied.

HARPAGON: Damn honour, damn you. Who put you up to it?

VALERE: Perhaps you mean what.

HARPAGON: Who who who?

VALERE: What? Well – Who? Since we're being fanciful, let me say a divinity, a god. And his name is Love.

HARPAGON: Love?

VALERE: Love.

HARPAGON: A lovely sort of love, he? Love of louis d'or, love of my doubloons.

VALERE: Ah no, your wealth doesn't come into it. Keep your wealth, so long as I retain the wealth already vouchsafed to me.

HARPAGON: The insolence. He asks me to let him keep what he's filched. Do let me steal from you, sir. Oh, thank you so much, sir, for letting me keep what I've stolen.

VALERE: You call it stealing?

HARPAGON: Yes yes, a theft of my heart, my soul, my treasure.

VALERE: A treasure, true, the most precious treasure imaginable. But it's a treasure I beg on my knees, this treasure that's pure gold. You have to give it to me.

HARPAGON: Have to – Give it –

VALERE: We've sworn a mutual vow, we've sealed a mutual promise never never never to be parted.

HARPAGON: Oh, a delightful vow, a most delectable promise.

VALERE: Committed to each other for ever and ever.

HARPAGON: Amen. I'll drive a coach and horses through your promise and your vow and your committal. Committal, eh? Commit him!

VALERE: Only death can drive us apart.

HARPAGON: Oh, you'll get that too, and a very nasty one.

VALERE: I've told you, sir, that it wasn't my intention to be pushed as far as I've been. My heart was racked by awareness of the apparent ignobility of my action, but my motives were altogether noble.

HARPAGON: Soon he'll be saying he stole my treasure from the purest of Christian charitable motives. But I'll put his Christianity right. I'll teach him his catechism.

VALERE: I'm ready to suffer. Pile of your punishments. Unleash your snakes and scorpions. But if wrong has been done and retribution has to be exacted, take note of this: your daughter is totally innocent.

HARPAGON: Oh yes, my daughter wouldn't be such a fool as to get herself embroiled. Leave her out of it. But tell me now, ingrate and treacherous villain, where is my treasure?

VALERE: Your treasure? With you still. Here in the house.

HARPAGON: Oh, my beloved. Not left the house, you say?

VALERE: Here as always.

HARPAGON: Not touched – Not laid a hand on – ?

VALERE: Me touch? Lay a hand on? We're speaking, sir, of a love ardent but respectable. Of a love immaculate and pure. Pure, yes, though I burn, I burn –

HARPAGON: Burn? You've burned my my my –

VALERE: Let me die rather than have shown your treasure the least hint of an impure desire, an impure thought. A treasure too wise, too self-respecting, too too –

HARPAGON: Self-respecting? My box too – ?

VALERE: My desires are bounded by a respect that is for the moment confined to the joy of my ardent eyes. I would never perform so criminal an act as to profane the passion that those beautiful eyes inspire.

HARPAGON: Got beautiful eyes now, has it? By God, I've seen love in my time, but I've still to take my money as a mistress. There are, so to speak, physical limits.

VALERE: Dame Claude, your servant, sir, knows all too well the sincerity of our avowals. Ask her to testify.

HARPAGON: So she's in it too, is she?

VALERE: Yes, sir, she knows it all. And it's she who finally persuaded your daughter to accede to my proposal, to join her heart to mine.

HARPAGON: He's so scared of the gallows that his mind's wandering. What the devil has my daughter to do with it?

VALERE: Your daughter, sir, has yielded to my long endeavours, to the strength of my passion, against the force of her own modesty. She accepts my love and returns it.

HARPAGON: What modesty? Whose modesty?

VALERE: Your daughter's. It's only since yesterday that she's compromised it sufficiently to accept my proposal and to agree to twine, sign, assign, consign her fate to mine.

HARPAGON: My daughter? You mean get married? To you?

VALERE: That's what I've been trying to say.

HARPAGON: Oh God! More disgrace!

JACQUES: *(To the* **SUPERINTENDENT.***)* Write it all down.

HARPAGON: Theft after theft. Crime after crime. Murder follows murder. Yes, sir, get it all down, make out the charge. A wretch and a thief on his own admission. Get a better pen.

VALERE: I won't have these names. And you'll take them back when you know who I am.

Scene Four

HARPAGON: Ah, here she is. Daughter unworthy of such a father. Is this how you put to proof the moral lessons I've tried to instil? To let yourself be taken in by the unholy lusts of an infamous thief? To get yourself engaged to him without your father knowing a thing about it? But you've made a big mistake, both of you. Four thick strong convent walls for you, my girl. And for you, a nice touch of the gallows will cool you down a bit.

VALERE: Anger is no fair judge. I'd better be heard before I'm condemned.

HARPAGON: Gallows, I said, gallows. And before the gallows – drawing and quartering. That'll put you right.

ELISE: *(On her knees.)*

Oh, father, show a little plain humanity.

Divest yourself of this – paternal vanity,

Subdue your feelings in a rational fashion

And think before you lash into a passion.

You act offended. How are we offensive?

Why should we two be guilty, apprehensive?

Think back to the eventualities

That fired the fuse that flamed and made me his,

That make me still alive and still your daughter –

That bad time when I plunged into the water

From a post-chaise drawn by a rabid horse

(A borrowed one – it wasn't ours, of course)

And Valère bravely saved me. I, and you,

Owe him my life. My life, and his life too,

Were altered by that salvatory swim.

Valère belongs to me, and I to him.

HARPAGON: That's nothing to the purpose. I have heard

Enough. And, daughter, I'd have much preferred

To see you drown than have you tied to one

Who's not a bit ashamed of what he's done.

Let justice take its course.

ELISE:		Soften your hard
	Heard. See reason.	
HARPAGON:		No.
JACQUES:	*(To* VALÈRE.*)*	You can regard
	The debt as fully paid.	
FROSINE:		A mad charade!

Scene Five

ANSELME: Monsieur Harpagon, you're not in a very hospitable condition. I'd better go.

HARPAGON: Ah, Signor Anselm –

ANSELME: I prefer Anselmo.

HARPAGON: You see in me the most wretched of human creatures. You've signed a marriage contract, and here's this ingrate of a girl who won't honour it. Honour, yes. She's stuck a knife in my honour, and just to add to it this thief, this traitor, posing as a servant, has robbed me. Yes, sliding into my life like oil, under the guise of a smiling smarmy major-domo, he robs me of my fortune and he corrupts my daughter.

VALERE: I'm sick of hearing of this robbery. I never went near your money.

HARPAGON: Marriage, they talk of marriage. This is an insult to you, Signor Anselm or Anselmo, as you prefer, and a smack in the face of the law. Well, you have the law on your side; and I recommend that you pursue the law to the limit.

ANSELME: Oh no. God forbid that I should be a party to a forced marriage and lay claim to a heart already given to another. But if it's your honour that seems to be in question, naturally I'll invoke the law.

HARPAGON: Well, here's the police superintendent, a good man who can write in a good round hand, ready to perform his office. Charge this villain, and have him taken away.

VALERE: I see. Loving your daughter is a crime.

     As for this gallows you bring up all the time,

     To see me off – love's sacrificial lamb –

     You'll hang yourself when you know who I am.

HARPAGON: Who you are, indeed. I know all about these thieves and rogues and scoundrels who get themselves up as dukes and marquises. Who do you say you are – the heir to the French throne?

VALERE: I lay no claim to anything in France.

     To Naples, yes. Despite this circumstance

     Of base imposture, I am quick to claim

     All Naples knows my family and my name.

ANSELME: All Naples, eh? Here's one who knows all Naples.

     Your family, then, belongs to the strong staples

     Of Neapolitan society?

     That claim's unlikely to impose on me.

VALERE: *(Proudly donning his hat.)*

     I defy your scepticism. You say you know

     All Naples. If that happens to be so,

     There's no doubt that you know who happens to be

     – Or to have been – Dom Thomas d'Alburcy.

ANSELME: Nobody knows him better, sir, than me.

HARPAGON: I don't give a damn about this Dom.

ANSELME: Excuse me, please. Let's hear him out. I'm rather

     Intrigued.

VALERE:	Dom Thomas d'Alburcy's my father.

Or was.

ANSELME: You mean that?

VALERE: Yes.

ANSELME: That will not wash.

Try another story. That one's bosh.

VALERE: I resent that. I can justify the claim.

ANSELME: Dom Thomas d'Alburcy's your father's name?

VALERE: Yes, I have proof.

ANSELME: Supreme audacity.

I can confound your story. Know that he,

The gentleman you speak of, died at sea,

Along with his wife and children, when they left

A Naples split by discord and bereft

Of decency and justice. Their escape

From fire and murder, robbery, rapine, rape

Was something to thank God for. But the sea

Exerted its own implacable cruelty.

And all this happened sixteen years ago.

VALERE: I confound your confoundation. You don't know

The total story. Of how a boy of seven,

His servant too, were, by the grace of heaven,

Saved from that shipwreck by a ship of Spain

Whose captain, moved by pity for the pain

The boy endured, brought him up as his own.

And when the boy was old enough, alone,

But educated in the soldier's arts,

He marched off boldly into foreign parts,

Including France, and made his way somehow.

This is the boy who's speaking to you now.

As for my orphan state – I ceased to grieve:

In my bereavement I could not believe.

My father dead – this I would not accept.

I searched for him and searched for him and kept

On searching for him – till the accident

Of the near-drowning of my loved one sent

My heart into a bliss of servitude

To beauty, goodness. From then I pursued

My father's whereabouts by proxy, since

The one-track heart that lovers all evince

Enforced my being here – a hypocrite,

A flatterer – but I do not blush for it,

For I was near my love.

ANSELME: What testimonies,

Apart from your own words, what witnesses

Can prove that this alleged truth truly is?

VALERE: The Spanish captain's still alive. I own

My father's jewels and an agate stone

My mother gave me dangles from my neck.

My servant too was salvaged from the wreck.

His name is Pedro. He's somewhere or other.

MARIANE: Heavens. I know it now. You are my brother.

VALERE: You are my sister?

MARIANE: Yes. I knew the eclipse

Of doubt on hearing all this from your lips.

My mother – oh, the ecstasy in store

For her, for you – a thousand times and more

Has told me the sad story of our loss –

Our name, our fortune, impaled on the cross

Of Naples's brutal history. But we too

Were saved from shipwreck, not alas, like you,

By Spanish angels. Devils rescued us,

Corsairs, pirates, bearded, villainous,

As we lay feebly on a floating spar.

And then, in an Algerian slave bazaar,

They sold us. Our Islamic master's knavery

Kept us for ten long years in wretched slavery,

But then he died. His daughter let us go.

So – back to Naples: nothing left to show

Our past prosperity. My father? No.

No news. And so to Genoa, Marseilles,

Searching and searching, searching all the way.

No news, no money, mother growing old,

Old and sick and hopeless. Our few gold

Trinkets kept us. But they're gone, all sold.

And that's our story.

ANSELME: But the story's told.

Done with. Finished. Heaven's blessings flow

On us poor mortals, who can sometimes know

The age of miracles is with us yet.

Come to my arms, my angels. Let's forget

The tribulations over. Let us rather

Rejoice. I've found my children.

VALERE: You're our father?

MARIANE: My mother's husband, whom she's wept so long for?

ANSELME: This is the moment heaven sings a song for.

I am your father, yes, my son, my daughter,

Dom Thomas d'Alburcy, who, on the water,

Safe with his treasure, somehow failed to perish

And, once ashore, lived sixteen years to cherish

A memory of happiness. Alas,

Memories aren't enough. I let time pass,

Returned to Naples, saw my hopes were finished,

My chance of reinstatement much diminished,

For enemies still sought to end my life.

I changed my name and settled here. A wife,

The chance of building a new family,

Of sweetening my exile, seemed to me

Right for a middle-aged philosophy.

But that's all over. Life is new begun.

HARPAGON: This one here. You say that he's your son?

ANESLME: My dear son.

HARPAGON: Right. I hold you responsible for the hundred thousand he's filched. Fetch that pen.

ANSELME: Stole it, did he?

HARPAGON: Stole it.

VALERE: Who says so?

HARPAGON: Master Jacques there.

VALERE: You said it, did you?

JACQUES: I said nothing.

HARPAGON: Here's the Superintendent, who took down his deposition.

VALERE: So – you still think me capable of so foul an action?

HARPAGON: Capable or not, I want my money back.

Scene Six

CLEANTE: Stop your accusations, father, and cease tormenting yourself and everybody else. I've found where it is and you can have it if you agree to my marriage with Mariane.

HARPAGON: Where is it?

CLEANTE: Don't worry. I know. The question is: do I marry Mariane and you get your strongbox back – or do we cancel the joint undertaking?

HARPAGON: Is anything gone from it?

CLEANTE: It's all there, bright as a wedding bell. Consent to our marriage and persuade Mariane's mother to consent – or at least leave her free to choose between prospective son-in-laws. And then you get it back.

MARIANE: There's more than a mother involved now. A father and a brother.

CLEANTE: What?

ANSELME: Heaven allows no man to set his face

Against a contract hallowed in that place.

So, Master Harpagon, don't raise your voice

Against a sweet and reasonable choice –

Young to the young. Give them no further trouble.

Let's have a wedding, and let's make it double.

HARPAGON: I want to see my box before I decide on a judgment.

CLEANTE: You'll see it safe and sound.

HARPAGON: You realise I have no money for a marriage settlement?

ANSELME: I've enough.

HARPAGON: And you'll pay all the expenses of this double wedding?

ANSELME: I will. Satisfied?

HARPAGON: I'll need special clothes for the occasion. Who's going to pay? I can't.

ANSELME: Leave it to me. Forget money and rejoice.

SUPERINTENDENT: Softly softly. Talking about forgetting money, who's paying the fee for the engrossing of the deposition?

HARPAGON: Nothing to do with me.

SUPERINTENDENT: Waste of time, waste of effort, waste of ink – and it's all got to be paid for.

HARPAGON: You've got a deposition. All you need is a prisoner. Take him and hang him.

JACQUES: Nice, isn't it? I get beaten for telling the truth and now I get hanged for lying.

ANSELME: I beg you to forget it, Master Harpagon. Why cast a blight on a day like this?

HARPAGON: You'll pay that too?

ANSELME: I'll pay.

> Let's spread the news. Paris is warm and sunny.
>
> The Paris markets drip with milk and honey.

THE COUPLES: We've got each other.

HARPAGON: And I've got my money.

THE END